# Dangerous Slopes

# Dangerous Slopes

Kenneth Janiec

authorHOUSE®

*AuthorHouse™ LLC*
*1663 Liberty Drive*
*Bloomington, IN 47403*
*www.authorhouse.com*
*Phone: 1-800-839-8640*

*Published by AuthorHouse   01/28/2014*

*ISBN: 978-1-4259-5789-6 (sc)*
*ISBN: 978-1-4918-5049-7 (e)*

To all the ski and snowboard instructors, ski patrollers, and resorts that make it safe and fun to ski; and to skiers who can't wait for the season to start and never want it to end.

# Chapter 1

The sky was blue, and the sun was bright. Coloradoans experience this weather at least three hundred days out of the year. Colorado gets more of these picture-perfect days than San Diego does.

Debbie and I moved to Denver from Fairfax, Virginia, ten years earlier. After spending a number of winter vacations skiing there, we fell in love with the area and made a calculated move. What I mean by a calculated move is that we calculated what we needed for the move, and we moved. There was no earth-shattering financial wizardry on our part—just old-fashioned emotions and gut feelings.

Having worked in the computer field a number of years after graduating from college, I was quickly able to get a job as a support engineer for a software-consulting firm in Denver. In my off time from being a database administrator, I was trying to build my own computer consulting business. My dream of having my own company was slowly developing before my eyes.

Debbie was a marketing specialist for another company in town, but her dream was to become an attorney. To make her dream come true, she enrolled in law school at the University of Denver as a part-time student. Three years later, she graduated and passed the Colorado bar exam on the first try. She worked as an attorney for a large downtown law firm. Our lives couldn't have been much better. We found a beautiful old craftsman-style home in Denver near our jobs. We were also close to a mall that had all our favorite stores.

We enjoyed summer hikes and winter skiing trips with friends in the mountains west of Denver. On one of those skiing trips, we decided to invest in a townhouse in Silverthorne, Colorado. It was only about eighty-five miles from our house in Denver, just west on I-70 toward the mountains. This highway passed through some of the most interesting terrain in the state, including the Continental Divide.

After signing the divorce papers in the morning, I'm now driving to the townhouse to make it my permanent home, while Debbie got the craftsman home in Denver. Knowing that the ski season opening day was a few weeks away, I spent the previous two weekends moving my personal stuff to a storage area in town. Unfortunately, the townhouse didn't have a basement, and I needed to organize my stuff. Debbie was always good in organizing stuff, but I had mediocre organizing skills. Even though I had built storage shelves in the garage, I still needed to rent a storage area. After signing the divorce papers in the morning, I stopped to get a bite to eat and took Stanley for a walk.

Stanley is a tri-color basset hound that we got as a puppy from a breeder in Boulder. We had basset hounds as children, and Stanley brought back so many wonderful memories. He was five years old, about fifty-five pounds, and just as playful as the day we had brought him home. After wiping his slobber off the windows and brushing his hair off the passenger seat, I was glad that Debbie had allowed me to keep him. I wasn't surprised. Since Debbie was in law school for a good part of his puppy years, he and I grew quite close. Debbie's law school classes, our parties, and nice trips didn't matter, but Stanley did.

I had someone to talk to. Stanley was a loyal friend, and that was fine with me.

# Chapter 2

I always enjoyed driving through the Eisenhower Tunnel. The two-mile tunnel was located about sixty-five miles west of Denver. The engineering marvel is the highest vehicle tunnel in the world with an elevation of about 11,000 feet. Two tunnels or bores running east to west had been cut through the Continental Divide at Loveland Pass. To the south, I could see skiers at Loveland Ski Resort.

One tunnel was finished in 1973, and the other was completed in 1979. I considered it the gateway to some of the biggest ski resorts in Colorado and, possibly, in North America. Traveling through the tunnel melted away my stresses. Boy, did I need that feeling right now.

Silverthorne had the same fast food chains, outlet stores, and gas stations as any thriving tourist town in America, but it was near the resorts in Breckenridge, Keystone, Copper, and Elks Run. Elks Run was my destination.

It was about twenty miles northwest from the main intersection in Silverthorne, through two mountains gulches, and over one pass within the Arapaho National Forest. On this crisp, blue-sky autumn day, I didn't care. Many of the Aspen trees had already shed their leaves. For the fall, they turned bright yellow.

The colors reminded me of a yellow fall bouquet and were different from the colors on the East Coast. The oak and maple trees usually turned red or orange. The smell of fallen leaves brought me back to helping my dad rake leaves in upstate New York. In those days, we were able to burn them. Mom, Dad, and I would sit on a couple of chairs and drink hot chocolate while taking in the scent of the burning leaves. I learned to ski in the Adirondacks, and I never stopped.

Debbie was from Long Island, New York, and we met in our college years. I thought about the times Debbie and I visited our parents in New York and their trips to our home in Virginia. My dad had passed away about five years earlier, and my mom wasn't able to travel, but we made a few trips to New York to visit her and Debbie's parents. Debbie got along with mom very well, and their marathon recipe-swiping sessions on the phone are classic. My mom took our divorce badly and added the wisdom of a good Irish mother. "It could be worse. You could have had children," she said.

Stanley looked like he needed to pee.

I said, "Stanley, we're almost there. Hang in there."

He looked at me with his basset hound eyes that made me feel bad about everything. When I looked away, he finally looked out the window.

I'm not crazy when I talk to Stanley. Anyone who owns a dog knows that you can talk to your dog as if they understand you. The best part is that you can talk to them in public, and the public doesn't mind. They even smile. I believe that dogs sort of know what we are saying.

A sign that extended over Main Street announced that the opening day of the ski season was just two weeks away because of the early snow and snow-making opportunities. Elks Run was a picture-perfect ski resort. Main Street had upscale shops and eateries, a gas station, and even a couple houses of worship. There were many condominiums, townhouses, and Victorian homes in town. Yes, it's a town. A few years earlier, the residents petitioned the county and the state legislature, and Elks Run was incorporated as a town. Nestled between Dillon Trail and Chief Mountain at the base of Buffalo Mountain, the area had wildflower-colored pastures in so many colors. Elks Run had bike trails, festivals, concerts, and a recreation center for full-time residents. Heck, it even had a full-time police department!

As we passed Gus's Ski and Bike Shop, a light snow began to fall. Putting on my wipers and defroster, I thought about the heavy wet snow from the East Coast. Shoveling that heavy, icy stuff was back-breaking work. The atmospheric conditions and dry humidity caused the Colorado snow to be light and fluffy. Many times, I used a broom to brush the snow off the stairs and sidewalks. There were twenty-six ski resorts in the state; Elks Run was the newest.

The developers of the resort took the best from all the Colorado ski resorts, including Vail, Copper Mountain, Steamboat, and Arapahoe

Basin. It has attitude and altitude. At 12,777 feet, it's one of the highest resorts, and *Ski and Snowboard* called it one of the top places to party. Maybe that was why I went there from another Colorado ski resort to work as a part-time ski and snowboard instructor. I taught adults how to do either one of the sports, but snowboarding was what I taught most of the time.

Snowboarding was taking off, and many adults wanted to learn. Even though I had been a ski instructor at other resorts, including a few on the East Coast, anyone who wanted to teach skiing at a resort needed to go through a boot camp where they evaluated your skiing or snowboarding skills. They also determined whether you have the, shall I say, eagerness to teach kids. Believe me, I love kids. When I was learning to ski at the tender age of six, the instructors were so nice and patient. I just don't like to chase them through the Ski School Children Hut or down the slope when they cannot stop. I don't want to take them to the bathroom or try to find their lost gloves while waiting for their parents to pick them up.

Debbie and I bought the townhouse so I could teach skiing over the weekends, develop my software consulting business, and get a free ski pass for her. I ended up teaching skiing part-time and developing my business, and I didn't have time to ski with Debbie. I guess two out of three wasn't too bad. When she started law school, she hardly came to the townhouse. Stanley and I were alone.

The road going to the resort starts at the end of town and does a two-mile ascent over a couple of streams and hair-raising switchbacks. Colorado has a number of mountain passes with roads that don't go straight up to the summits. The roads climb gradually. It's not a true straight climb. Turns are necessary. To make a right turn on an ascent, you need to turn ninety degrees to the right. The left turn is the same way, hence the name switchback. There are a few one hundred eighty-degree turns thrown in for good measure. I think the Colorado Department of Transportation (CDOT) road engineers built the roads that way to save the trees and to slow everyone down. They act like big speed bumps because many of these roads don't have guardrails. On the way up, I saw a Chinook twin-rotor helicopter with a big bucket carrying materials for the tower bases that would anchor the ski lift towers in place.

Elks Run was building a gondola chairlift. The world's highest and longest cable car system is in Venezuela. A French company built the

Teleférico in the late 1950s. It started out in Mérida at 5,172 feet and continued for nearly eight miles to the top of Pico Espejo (15,630 feet), the second-highest peak in Venezuela. The 10,457-foot climb covers four dramatic stages and takes an hour. There isn't skiing at the top, just sightseeing. For one reason or another, it's common for one or all sections to be shut for weeks. The Elks Run gondola would use a new lift system with a number of built-in monitoring systems. It would monitor and show the information on a computer screen, which would prevent it from having so many maintenance issues.

The huge lift was going to be an impressive undertaking. At some sections of the mountain, the lift towers hung the gondolas over one hundred feet off the mountain base; at some points, they were completely horizontal to the mountain. I can't understand why they were still working so late in the fall since frosty nights showed up quickly in this part of the state. It seemed unusual to me.

Nevertheless, with the dedication of this lift to Elks Run highest summit from the base lodge and the best back bowl skiing in Colorado around Presidents Day, I guess the work needed to be completed before the big snows. I kept driving so I wouldn't miss the beginning of the resort's seasonal employee meeting, could meet my old ski friends, and would get my uniform before they ran out of sizes that fit me.

Because basset hounds do not jump from cars, trucks, or any vehicle besides possibly go-karts, I opened the passenger door, picked Stanley up from the seat, and set him down on the ground. He was so happy to be on the ground that he awarded me with one of his marathon pee stops.

It was starting to snow more heavily and was not conducive to hanging out. We made our way quickly to the employee meeting.

# Chapter 3

Every ski season brings familiar faces back to the resort. I had seen many on the slopes and remembered their styles of skiing or snowboarding. That was how I remembered names.

Ski resort employees are a tight knit family, and none are tighter than ski instructors and patrollers. I could compare it to the Marine Corps esprit de corps. Since I worked as both, the testing was pretty intense. Ski patrollers had open ski clinics toward the end of the season; if you were chosen, you would usually need to attend classes during the entire summer, a few days per week. You learned advanced first aid and how to transport an injured skier correctly in the toboggan.

During the ski season, the skills learned during the summer classes were used on the slopes, including how to extract skiers stuck on the chairlifts or gondolas. Usually, the evaluation process for a ski instructor took about three days. One of those days was spent skiing, snowboarding, or maybe both. Knowing how to ski and snowboard was a plus. The evaluation consisted of how well you could ski on the resort's blue-and-black diamond terrain and whether you had the proper skiing technique for that terrain.

We needed to ski, turn, and execute a number of maneuvers. Many didn't make the cut and just wanted to say they had tried out for a position. Those who showed some promise continued. All resorts needed children instructors. The best skiing instructors had the opportunity to teach teenagers and adults, but those who needed a little more practice— if they were friendly and outgoing—started out by teaching children. Don't get me wrong; some actually volunteered for that job. They spent time interviewing with several evaluators who asked questions about teaching preferences (if that really matters) and then gave a series of what-if scenarios. For instance, what if I had five adult students in an intermediate skiing class and four of them are doing really well, but one is not getting it. The other students were getting bored because you were taking time with the one student. What should you do? Do you tell him that he should not try skiing again and should just go back to the lodge and read a book?

Since I really did want to get the job, I told the student to register for a basic beginner's class to brush up on the basics of turning and stopping. That is how the evaluators see if you can communicate clearly. Heck, there have been skiers that could ski and snowboard better than I could, but they just couldn't communicate with other students. The resorts want friendly, helpful employees who make guests want to come back.

After working as a part-time instructor for a season and getting a sign-off from the resort's training ski instructor, I was eligible to join the Professional Ski Instructors Association (PSIA). The American Association of Snowboard Instructors (AASI) is an arm of it. There have been issues between the skiing and snowboard instructors about who is better. They are both under the PSIA organization, split in two professional organizations known as the PSIA/AASI. There are yearly dues, and both organizations require certification every couple of years and testing for advanced instructor levels. Your hourly rate goes up with each level of experience, and you must stay certified by taking the required courses ever couple of seasons. The skiing and snowboard levels for students have development phases from level one through nine, the expert level. Some instructors have expanded their teaching skills to groomed, powder, bumps, half-pipe, park, and freestyle skiing. This translates into more money and more students.

Elks Run requires us to cover the techniques in the skiing and snowboard manuals and make sure our students had a fun, safe time on the slopes. Being humorous on the slopes can help relax frazzled students and differentiate one resort from another. The happiest instructors worked at these resorts, and the word about the resorts spread quickly. I worked with instructors in their twenties, thirties, forties, fifties, and sixties.

We were good on the slopes, liked snow, and had fun with our students. Let's face it, when a family of four spends over fifteen hundred dollars for transportation, a week of lessons and staying at a condominium, it made sense to teach a lesson where they learned and had fun.

The instructors who reach the expert levels are very good and usually are the full-time instructors who work every day. At a well-known resort, this means more money for the season. For a part-timer like me, I made up to $1,200 for the required twenty days of work. The higher hourly rate was more for full-timers who had developed a client base and usually came back every year for brush-up lessons. These clients passed their recommendations on to family and friends. As part-time instructors, we taught anyone who signed up for a class. The full-time instructors usually got the private lessons. I was a level-two snowboard instructor and was looking for time to certify for third level, the highest level.

I liked to bring Stanley to these meetings and the locker room. He brought so many smiles. The women really liked him. Stanley allowed me to practice my "can I get to know you" lines. I would get a laugh from some or an eye roll from the others. With resort employees, word travels at the speed of an avalanche, and we needed to very careful about what we said or did. It may not make the resort's employee newsletter, but your name will pop up on the slopes like new snow if you date or have an affair with another instructor. That has happened to few good people while indirectly affecting a few others. It may not be the same in other seasonal jobs, but it's normal in this one. The physical aspect of skiing, boarding, partying, working out, and being in good shape made us want sex.

I prided myself in not having my marriage break up in that way, but being on the outside of that circle really didn't help save it.

# Chapter 4

It took a good five minutes of everyone rubbing and stroking Stanley's head and ears before we sat down next to Ron Gustaff. Ron and I went back a number of years to a few ski resorts in Colorado when we started as instructors and had followed each other right to Elks Run. He and his wife owned Gus's Ski and Bike Shop, which everyone passed on the way up to the resort.

Ron was slim and tall with a bushy black mustache and hair to match.

"Hey, Ron, it's so good to see you."

"Oh, Mike. It's so good to see you too!"

We shook hands, gave each other a hug, and sat down. "Mike, I'm sorry about you and Debbie. I know you mentioned it to me a few months ago, and all I can say is that Ginny and I are very sorry."

"Yes, today was the day. I guess Stanley and I are together from here on out."

Ron dropped to his knees while Stanley rolled on his back to get a belly rub from him.

Debbie and I had always enjoyed Ron and Ginny and considered them our very best friends. Before Debbie started law school, we spent many summer and winter weekends enjoying the splendors of Colorado by hiking, mountain biking, and visiting some very unusual places. When Ron's business started taking off, we followed Ron as he took tourists on summer bike tours in Summit County. He met Ginny when they were going to the University of Colorado. He graduated with a hotel and restaurant management degree, and Ginny with a marketing degree.

They had dreamed of owning a business in Colorado and worked for a number of regional sports companies. Ron became a regional VP for one of those companies, and Ginny was the marketing director. Since Ron visited many areas of the state, he found that Elks Run was recruiting small businesses. Ron and Ginny pooled their savings and Gus's Ski and Bike Shop was born five years ago, the same year they married. They started doing so well that Ron was one of the first businesses where I installed a software business suite to help them manage the inventory. I guess it was an easy sell because of our close friendship. They lived in a log home about ten miles northwest of the resort, overlooking a valley. The idyllic setting was one of the best homes in the valley.

The employee meeting started in the resort's main dining room of Heavenly Lodge with Betty Owens, director of personnel, introducing Joe Bunn, president and CEO of Elks Run Resort. She was a petite, tanned, brown-haired woman who defied aging. She explained that she was happy to have us working at one the best and newest resorts in Colorado. Western Venture owned Elks Run as well as resorts in California, Vermont, British Columbia, and Switzerland. Last year, I had read in the employee monthly newsletter and on his Facebook page that Joe Bunn had worked his way up in Western Ventures, the parent company. He was fifty-four and lived in an exclusive area near the resort. They enjoyed skiing and had a daughter who had graduated from an Ivy League school on the East Coast. She was the assistant to the director of marketing and conveniently lived in a condominium within the resort.

Joe Bunn told us how we had set the record for most skier visits of any resort in Colorado for the past three years; with the new gondola lift addition, the resort should beat all records for the coming years. It would be the first twelve-person gondola in the country and, possibly, in the world.

When Ron and I traveled to Steamboat for a PSIA and AASI certification, we rode our first eight-person gondola. It was impressive. We felt that we were skiing somewhere in the Alps. Skiers with disabilities attached their special skis to the outsides of the gondolas, but we walked on and off with our skis or snowboards. It was a great way to transport people to the top of the mountain.

The name of the new gondola lift will be Blue Sky. When it is ready, it would take skiers to the top of Summit County from the base lodge, an elevation of 12,777 feet. Then, they'd be able to ski both the back and front bowls. In resort language, bowls are half-coffee cups with fairly steep sides that guide the skiers to the bottom. The east front bowl would face the main resort, and guests could see skiers ski down the bowl on blue and a few back diamond trails.

At the bottom of the front bowl, Eastway lift, a quad lift, would take them back to the top of the bowl. The west back bowl would have a few more black diamond steep drops, and a quad lift named Westside would bring skiers back to the top. Guests could ski all day in the bowls and not come down to the main base lodge until the end of the day. Clouds Lodge was on top of both bowls, and it offered lattes dining, and views of beautiful Summit County.

Joe also said that all returning employees would be receiving a 15 percent raise at the start of the season. Everyone cheered and applauded the good news.

Rising global warming temperatures were causing many lower-altitude ski resorts to shut down because they couldn't afford to invest in snowmaking machinery. That was why a capital-rich company like Western Ventures could go on a purchasing or expansion spree. It gave them a four-season playground to reduce any dependence on snowfall in one area. Colorado and the Rockies were excellent areas to run and expand a resort.

Joe covered the ambitious plan to expand the resort's condominium development. This included adding a hundred condominiums starting at around three hundred thousand dollars and employee housing. That statement brought loud applause from a majority of the employees. During the winter months, many employees traveled dangerous roads and passes, making it a stressful drive to work. CDOT does a great job of keeping the roads and passes clear and safe, but we couldn't help but think about the drive to and from the resort when it snowed.

Joe was hoping for approval of the master plan and a building permit from the Forest Service. The permit process has been an ongoing thorny issue in Colorado and the West. A few environmental groups have been battling ski resorts and their plans to expand areas. All ski areas lease the land from the Forest Service for a nominal fee. Elks Run needed to submit another plan to the Forest Service for the planned expansion. To keep the needs of the community, general public, and environmental issues in balance, the Forest Service allowed residents to voice any concerns at various open meetings.

Environmental groups attended the meetings to express their concerns and present their facts. I never went to the meetings, but I heard that they were very lively. Each side pointed a finger at the other about who was right. Based upon the meetings, research, and the resort's plan, the Forest Service would make the decision on the permit.

The Forest Service approved the permit for the gondola with additional land allocated to the resort, but not until after an environmental group named PineTree had caused so much chaos that, the state police and the sheriff's department had to be called in to stop the road blockades, vandalism, and fighting. It was scary for everyone who worked at the resort. Since law enforcement officials thought that the group was receiving money and assistance from other groups within the United States, the FBI investigated them. I didn't think the disagreements would ever go away.

Joe Bunn hoped the Forest Service and the local residents would approve the newest plan. He turned the meeting back to Betty Owens, and she started talking to the newly hired employees.

I tugged on Ron's jacket. I told him that I needed to take a break and asked him to watch Stanley for a few minutes. I'd come back with a few bottles of water. He gave me a thumbs-up. As I made my way to the back of the room, I nodded to a few of my friends.

Joe came up to me and said, "Mike Doyle, welcome back!"

"Thanks, Mr. Bunn."

"I wanted to have my secretary call you, but I thought I would see you here. My management team liked your proposal for managing our resort databases, and they accepted it."

"That's just great," I said. I was shocked; this contract would be my first big one, and I never thought I had a chance.

"I'm having a management meeting on Monday morning at ten. I would like you to attend and have my staff meet you. Just give Janet a call to let her know that you'll be there," he said.

"Sure, I'll be there, and I'll let Janet know. Thanks again."

"Great, see you there," he said as he turned toward another employee.

*Wow, can this be true? I started the day on a sad note, got better driving here, and now it turns out good for both Stanley and me. Since, I handed in my resignation to my former employer, if I can be so lucky and land a few more big contracts. I forgot what I wanted to do. Oh yes, get some bottled water.*

"Hey Ron, did I miss anything important?"

"No, the same stuff. However, we are getting new jacket and bib ski pants this year. They're from Spyder."

"Great. I have some other good news for you. I got the contract to manage the resort databases."

"That is great! When do you start?"

"I need to go to a management meeting this Monday. I guess they'll hand over notes and all that stuff."

"Aren't you full of good news today? By the way, I think Stanley wants some water."

Stanley looked up at me. "Oh, Stanley, I forgot. Sorry." I handed Ron his water.

Stanley drank from the water bottle. When Debbie and I took him for walks, we always carried water bottles with us. We had a special canteen with a bowl attached to it. I just took the strap and looped over my shoulder. I guess he saw us drink out of our water bottles and thought that was the way to do it. He probably thought it was faster to lap it from the end of the bottle.

I focused my attention on Betty's presentation. She ended by thanking everyone for attending the meeting on such a cold, snowy day and asked that the new full-time and part-time employees stayed while the others picked up their uniforms.

After picking my jacket and the ski bib overalls, I stopped by an office to get my picture ID taken. I went to the locker room. Luckily, the resort's main lodge and the administration offices are joined by covered walkways, and the walk was quick. Well, sort of. Stanley drew the attention of many people along the way, including a favorite dog stop between each building. I forgot that the resort's computer room was in the basement of that building. I had never paid attention to the descending stairs and the sign that said "IT Department." I needed to know where it was located for Monday's meeting.

The ski instructors' locker room contained lockers for about twenty full-time and twenty-five part-time instructors. During the winter season, the space was at a premium. Ron and I had shared lockers for as long as we had been instructors. When we arrived, Ron was setting a new four-digit combination. He knew how to pack a locker.

There were a few myths that circulated around this locker room. The first myth said that ski instructors were honest. I wouldn't want a good person to go bad. We always locked our locker and our skis and snowboards whenever they weren't in our hands. The second myth was that there were separate lockers for male and female instructors. Nope— we get dressed in front of the lockers. However, we limited the show-and-tell dressing to stripping down to our thermal underwear. No orgies in there, but it did let the mind go wild.

After Ron told me the combination, I put a bag of dog cookies on one of the top shelves for Stanley. I gave him one or two for sitting, we got our work schedules from the instructors' big white board, and we headed for the door to go home. Ron said good-bye to Stanley, and I said that I'd see him sometime during the week. We wished each other safe trips down the pass, knowing that the beautiful pass in the summer could be treacherous in the winter.

After we walked through about two inches of new snow—on top of the four inches on the ground—Stanley and I arrived at the truck. Waiting for the windshield to defrost, I switched on the radio and listened to the weather forecast. The weather was normal for that time of year: a high in the upper thirties, plenty of sun, and a chance of snow.

The road looked icy, and I switched to four-wheel drive and headed down the pass.

# Chapter 5

As I was driving down to Elks Run, I passed a number of trucks on the opposite side of the road. They were pulling trailers with the gondolas for the new Blue Sky lift. I started thinking about how the ski lift was going to change the resort and the lives of many people. There were times when I'd get a premonition that I couldn't explain, but I knew that something would happen. It could be a good or bad omen, but something would happen. I had that feeling.

I pulled into the garage and left the door open so Stanley and I could take a short walk. Looking up at the snow on the roof, I was happy to be safely home, but I was a little sad that Debbie was no longer part of our lives. We walked up the eight steps to the kitchen. Stanley never had a problem getting up those stairs, especially when it was time for dinner.

I was hungry, but Stanley came first. After his meal, I made a roast beef sandwich on rye with a kosher pickle and switched on the local news. The station switched to an interview with Joe Buns.

The reporter asked, "Mr. Bunn, I know the Colorado and Elks Run are excited to see and ride the new gondola ski lift. Will it be ready for Washington's Birthday weekend, and are you as excited as all of us?"

"Joan, I must say that I'm extremely excited for the entire State of Colorado and to all our skiers in Summit County about giving them one of the most sophisticated twelve-person gondolas in this state and the country. By the way, the gondola doesn't stop after our winter season; this lift will be available during the summer months so that everyone, including hikers and mountain bikers, will be able to enjoy the beautiful views of Elks Run and Buffalo Mountain."

"Isn't it true that you may be pushing the envelope in getting the lift ready for that weekend? I guess the question on everyone's mind is whether the cold weather will be detrimental in completing it."

"I can assure you that Brian Jones, our facilities and engineering manager, is working with the lift manufacturer and their designers on a daily basis to make sure that every step that they take to install it is both practical and safe. I can say that if it wasn't safe, we may have to delay the opening. However, that isn't going to happen because he has assured me that everything is on schedule. By the way, I would love to see Channel 7 News join us at our opening celebration."

"Mr. Bunn, we'll do our best to be there. Thanks for your time. Well, you heard it. It looks as though skiers and summer riders will be enjoying Colorado's newest and largest gondola starting this Washington's Birthday weekend. From Colorado's newest ski resort, Elks Run in Summit County, Colorado, this is Joan Edwards, Eyewitness News 7."

I clicked off the TV, put on a CD, and finished my sandwich. I could not imagine that the lift would be finished in time because of the surprisingly early cold weather in the middle of November. It just didn't seem logical to me, but I am not an engineer.

I checked my messages and had one from a sporting goods business that was interested in new software. On the business side of my life, I was two for two.

There was also a message from Debbie. "Hi Mike and Stanley. Today I got some mail delivered for you. I'm in the process of mailing it to you in an oversized envelope. If you forgot anything, just leave a message. It snowed a little here today. Say hello to Stanley for me. Bye."

It had been a long day. I said, "Stanley, let's go outside for short walk before turning in."

# Chapter 6

Waking up, the snow gauge on the balcony showed another five inches of new snow on top of the eight that had been there at bedtime. Sweeping the snow off the balcony, I spotted the local paper about ten feet from the garage door. The fast-falling snow probably caused the guy to fling it from the road.

Opening the garage door, Stanley darted off and bounced in the snow for about twenty feet. He stopped and waited for me to chase him. I made a snowball and tossed it to him, which disintegrated in his mouth as he tried to catch it.

While unrolling the paper and sitting down to eat at the breakfast nook, I glanced around the room. I liked the fact that the kitchen and the family room were together. It made it look and feel spacious. In addition, I liked the loft above the kitchen. This was the office where all my personal computers and servers connected to the fiber optic DSL line. A few of my customers allowed me to connect to their computers with a remote software package, which helped me diagnose and maintain their software.

A few years earlier, I had painted the loft with warm, earthy colors that were pleasing to the eye and brought out the Colorado outdoors. The furnishings were antiques and artifacts that Debbie and I had bought during our travels. I had a dry-ice refrigerator from 1902. I had to admit that I was not a decorator or art purchaser, and Debbie did a great job. I'm going to miss those trips with her. *Wow, I have to get those thoughts out of my mind, but I guess it's only natural that they do come to mind in familiar places. Who knows, she may be having these same thoughts.*

During the next couple of days, I had to meet with prospective clients, work out at the recreation center gym, pick up a few things at the grocery, and get some rest for that all-important meeting with the management staff. I was tired from thinking about all that stuff. I still couldn't believe that I had the contract to manage the Elks Run computers. Like any computer geek, I was interested in finding out how the information was stored and processed. After breakfast, it was time to take Stanley for a walk.

"Okay, Stanley, after our walk, you need to watch the house, play with your toys, or sleep—whatever comes first—while I start doing some of those errands."

# Chapter 7

Monday morning was cold and crisp; the temperature was around twenty-seven. Stanley and I took a long walk, said hello to our neighbors who had braved the weather, and took a good twenty-five-yard jog home. I felt good that he'd be all right until I get home. As the sun began to rise over the mountains, I headed to my meeting with Joe and his staff.

On the way to town, I passed a few red foxes and a white-tailed deer. I planned on stopping at the Coffee Cup Café in the center of town for a cup of Sumatra coffee and a pound of roasted espresso beans.

Jeff was behind the counter, and the usual locals were at the tables. I saw Pete Snow and his guide dog. Pete was sixty-five. He had been blinded from a mine accident in Leadville. Leadville, the highest town in the USA at 10,120 feet, was one of the most productive silver mines in Colorado and the nation at the turn of the nineteenth century.

Because of Stanley, I always carried at least two dog treats in my pockets. After saying hello to Pete, I asked him whether I could give Rusty a treat. Rusty, a seven-year-old Golden Retriever, was the second dog Pete had owned. Pete told me that you should never give a service dog anything without the permission of its owner. I wish I could say that for Stanley; he takes treats from anyone before I say anything. Pete said it was fine.

Rusty enjoyed the treat and wagged his tail.

Ron and Ginny walked in for their usual coffee and town gossip before opening their shop. Ron surprised me from behind and wrapped his arms around me in a bear hug. With a quick upward force of my hands and a twist of my body, I tried to get out of it, hoping that I don't knock over a table or two. We shook hands, and I gave Ginny a big hug.

"How're you guys doing this morning?"

Ron said, "Just great, Mike."

Ginny was tall, slim, and blonde. She wore jeans and a blue turtleneck sweater. "Mike, are you having that big management meeting today?"

"Yes. Since I don't know how long it will take, I jogged Stanley a little further today to get him ready for a longer day at home."

"Mike, Ron told me about your contract, and I think that's so great."

"Thanks. Before I forget, can I drop Stanley off at the shop tomorrow with his food and everything?"

"Sure, I'll let Mary know because she'll be opening tomorrow morning."

"Thanks, Ginny. Ron, did you see Joe on TV last night? Do you think the gondola lift will be completed in time?"

"I don't really know. A few guys in the facilities workshop said they doubt this thing could be pulled off by then."

"I think I agree with them. I don't think I want to be the first one to ride the lift on opening day—and maybe that whole week."

"You and I both, Mike."

"Thanks, Jeff," I said after picking up my coffee and beans. "Hey guys, I need to get going. I'll see you later."

As I opened the door to leave, I saw Bob Trent. He was one of two police officers in town. Bob was a big person with a larger smile. He had bushy silver hair and a moustache to go with it. He had been a police sergeant in Austin, Texas.

After taking a number of vacations to Colorado with his family, he and his wife moved there a couple of weeks after his retirement. He needed to get away from the heat and humidity of that place, and he had been smart enough to purchase a couple of acres of land outside of Elks Run. His log home sits on the property, and they brought along their horses. Their children and grandchildren love to visit.

"Hi, Bob," I said as we shook hands. "How has your day been so far? And how is Jodi?"

"Oh, the day and Jodi are just peachy," he said with a Texas accent. "Pretty soon, the season will begin, and it'll start getting a little busy and interesting. Are you and that ferocious hound dog looking forward to ski season?"

"You bet," I said with a smile. "Have a safe day, Bob."

"Thanks, you too. And I'll tell Jodi you asked about her."

I got into my truck and drove toward the resort.

Plowing the road made the pass relatively safe. You just need to take it slow. I saw and heard a scurry of activity from helicopters overhead. Passing an open trailhead, I saw a number of trucks parked with gondolas on them. With no cars behind me, I slowed down, pulled off the road, and reached for my binoculars. The cranes were unloading the gondolas onto skids pulled by bulldozers with special spiked wheels. The skids were taken to a cleared area so that the Chinook helicopter could lift them to the base lodge.

In the distance, I saw cement lifted by another helicopter and being poured in an area that was probably the base for one of the towers. A few of the workers in orange bib overalls waved, and I waved back. Getting back into my truck, the outdoor thermometer gauge on my display read thirty degrees.

At the resort, a sign explained the ski area parking was straight ahead; there was a separate sign for condominiums and townhouses. When I started as a part-time instructor three years earlier, there had only been three real estate developments. Now, it was up to five, and there was a gate with a security guard. I parked in a visitor's space. Since I didn't know where the conference room was located, I asked the receptionist at the front desk.

I reached the room with ten minutes to spare. I was proud that I had arrived early because I had a tendency to arrive at meetings right on time or a few minutes late. I ran out of excuses for being late. I sometimes used Stanley as an excuse, but no one believed me, didn't know what a basset hound was, or was too embarrassed to ask.

The door was open, and I walked into the room. Everyone looked up and smiled at me. The first one to greet me and shake my hand was Betty Owens. As the director of HR, she knew my name. I didn't know that the directors had received a letter announcing my hiring, position, and a little biography of me.

Betty introduced me to Joe Bunn's staff as I shook their hands. I sat down in a seat that had a great view of the main ski lodge and lift area. The snow looked great.

At 10:00 on the dot, Joe walked in with his secretary. He greeted me and asked whether everyone had introduced themselves. He started the meeting by having everyone brief me on their departments and the resort's database and any problems they'd had with their data.

I took notes for each area and was surprised when Brian Jones mentioned that the facilities and engineering department had temperature and motion sensors on all the lift stations and towers and throughout the mountain for earthquake and mountain-shifting analysis. These towers held the chairs and the new gondola cars. It was a very sophisticated system.

As a database administrator, I was hardly involved with the day-to-day activities of the applications that run on any database. I just worried about the database. I decided to start reading about current ski resort software. If I made recommendations to the staff, my value to the resort would increase. Yes, like a politician, I needed to plan for the next campaign or, in my case, a contract renewal.

Joe gave me a binder with recent documentation and a five-digit code for the computer room. He told me about the last contractor who had set up the database and the application programs. "Mike, again, if you need any additional information from my staff or you need to tell them about any issues that happened or will happen, then send an e-mail, phone, or knock on their doors. During the season, I like to have meetings using Skype. Janet will let you know the days and times. However, as critical as this information is for the resort, my door is always open to you. I can certainly find the time to fit you in my schedule. Welcome aboard!"

"Thank you, Mr. Bunn. It is a pleasure meeting all of you," I said. I gathered my notes and the binder, put them in my backpack, and quickly left the room.

# Chapter 8

As I left the room, it felt great to be part of the people who were responsible for running the resort. It was a huge responsibility, and I liked it.

I called Gus's Shop, and Mary answered the phone. "Hi, Mary. How's Stanley doing?" I asked.

"Oh, he's doing great and has even made some sales for me," she said.

"Hey, that's great. I need to spend another two hours at the resort before I can pick him up. Is that okay?"

"Sure. I probably won't be here, but I'll tell Ginny."

"Yes, let her know. If there is a problem, she can call my cell."

"Will do."

Since there wasn't anyone waiting at the main lodge restaurant's takeout window, I grabbed some takeout. In a few more days, it'll really be busy. When I reached the computer room, I entered the five-digit code and opened the door. The room had no windows and had two cubicles that were back to back to each other with plenty of space and great lighting. Each cubicle had a twenty-seven-inch flat-screen computer monitor, an ergonomic keyboard, and a large desk area. The floors were earth-tone granite and matched the color of the room. The desk chairs were very plush. I noticed the walls had black-and-white photos of the resort taken both in the daytime and at night. They were great photos. One of the walls had bookshelves with the documented information of the databases and the supported applications.

The databases were loaded on a Solaris-Oracle Exalogic Elastic Cloud X3-2 hardware system containing four nodes (eight of a full rack), each with its own ZFS Storage Appliance. The rack stands about seventy-eight inches tall with space to add up to thirty additional nodes. It weighs about 880 pounds and sits between the two cubicles. The system had Linux-Oracle operating system (O/S) pre-installed on it. The last contractor loaded Oracle databases on two different nodes. One node was the primary database, and the other was a standby database. This provided data-redundancy. If the primary database went down on one server, the other standby database on the other server would be able to come online with a few commands. The best part was that each database had the same information. The primary database sent the data to its standby database by a network connection. This connection was, rightly called "the heartbeat connection." This was a great system. No, it was a terrific system. I read the database architecture information and reviewed the diagrams that showed me how it all flowed together. I was impressed. The documentation was better than I read in some of the other companies I worked for in the past. I looked at the clock and saw that it was getting close to two o'clock. It had been a long day, and the ski season would open tomorrow.

I called Ginny at the shop and left a voice message saying that I was leaving the resort and would pick Stanley up in about thirty minutes. On the way down the pass, it started to snow. I felt good about this job and the beginning of the ski season. I wished Debbie were there with me to share this feeling. As I entered the shop, Stanley saw me. He ran toward me as I dropped down to my knees to meet him. After endless hugs, licks, and moans from him, I saw both Ron and Ginny out of the corner of my eyes. After giving Ginny a hug, I told them about my meeting. "Mike, that sounds so great for both you and the resort," Ron said.

Ginny said, "Mike, it looks as though you're going to have a very busy season and year."

"You bet."

Ginny reminded us that we needed to be ready for the start of the ski season tomorrow. I agreed and said that I was stopping by in the morning to drop Stanley off.

Ginny asked whether she could take Stanley to the town's business owners at the town hall.

"Sure, Ginny. No problem," I said.

"That's great. They always enjoy seeing Stanley, and the meeting goes faster because they want to play with him. We forget what we are there for," she said with a smile.

I took Stanley for a brief walk down the deserted street to my truck. I liked the way the gaslights lit up the streets around town. It reminded me of how my parents described Central Park in New York City on a cold night.

# Chapter 9

Before locking the house, I put a bag of Stanley's dry food in the truck and took him for a walk. Opening day was always a crazy scene. The Coffee Cup Café and other restaurants were packed. Pete and Rusty enjoyed the mix of customers at the café. He liked talking to people. It was a tradition for resort openings to attract teenagers and grownups. Conveniently, many of the opening-day skiers become sick or skipped school and work. I liked being a ski instructor during this time.

In the parking lot at Gus's shop, I walked Stanley through the rear door. There was a line of customers waiting to rent skis and snowboards. The season has started for Gus and Ginny, and I was very happy to see the store busy again.

"Ginny, good morning,"

"Good morning, Mike. Hello, Stanley," Ginny said as she got down on her knees to rub his head and long ears. In return, she got a big tail wag and a lick of her face. "Well, Stanley, it looks as though you haven't lost your touch with women like your dad has," she said.

"Oh, you know how to hurt a guy." I walked back to the truck to get Stanley's food. While waiting for Stanley to finish his breakfast, Ginny asked me to answer a customer's question about snowboards. When the customer found out that I was a snowboard instructor at Elks Run, he said that he'd ask for me for a private snowboard lesson.

I gave him my card and gave Ginny a wink. "Ginny, I need to go. Did Ron have an earlier lesson today?"

"Yes, you missed him by thirty minutes. I believe he was going to get breakfast at the resort cafeteria," she said.

"Stanley, be a good boy and guard Ginny, okay?" I said with a smile.

"He always does," she said.

Stanley was wagging his tail.

I gave her a quick hug. "I may be back after the store closes; because I need to check on the resort databases."

"That shouldn't be a problem. Just knock on the back door as usual. Keep an eye out for Ron, okay?"

"You bet I will," I said. I left the shop and started driving to the resort.

# Chapter 10

The trip to the resort was slower than usual because of the opening-day traffic. The parking lots were almost full. Driving past the main lodge, I saw the local TV stations and a live radio broadcast. A TV station was giving out free hot chocolate and cookies.

I turned into the gated employee parking lot, showed my employee badge to the attendant, and pulled into a spot. Lowering the tailgate, I got my board and backpack. I left my skis locked in the back because I'd likely be teaching snowboarding.

I walked into the locker room, said my hellos, and put my board in the rack. I saw some new boards and a few battered veterans. My board fell in between those boards, and I loved it. My work board was an F2 Flame, 160 centimeters long with step-in soft bindings. I loved putting on my Burton "Work Force" boots. With a pair of moisture-wicking calf socks, they felt so good. I compared them to putting on my Minnetonka moccasins and wearing them on the slopes. My racing board was a Dynastar "Course de Monde," 163 centimeters with step-in hard bindings. With those types of bindings, I needed to put on hard boots and would lock them to the board. The boots were similar to those worn by skiers and were more restrictive then my soft boots. When I made the slightest foot correction, my board would follow. This was critical in skiing and snowboard racing. The soft-binding boots were more forgiving.

In the locker, Ron left a note that said he had a lesson with Dr. Benson. He had left the lunches Ginny made for both of us in the refrigerator with our names on them. I was really lucky to have them as friends. Dr. Benson has been Ron's opening-day first lesson for the past three seasons. He was about eighty, a retired surgeon, and a very good skier. He skied National Standard Race (NASTAR) "King of the Mountain" races and was ranked third in the country for his age.

Looking at my watch, I had ten minutes to get dressed and not enough time to make a quick warm-up run down Squaw Trail. It was right under the main quad lift, Skyway. I made my way to the morning assignment area. The instructor assignment area was near the beginner-intermediate lift, Stairwell, which was a short walk or run from the instructor lockers. If you start out in time, it's a walk. That morning, it was not a walk.

After grabbing an instructor radio from the rack and swiping my employee ID through the timecard clock, I slung my board over my back and ran like hell to the area.

Seeing my boss, I said, "Good Morning, Cathy. How's the morning going?"

"Hey, Mike. I see you are back for another tortuous year with me." She began writing the names of the snowboard instructors present. Cathy had started snowboarding when girls weren't seen doing the sport, and she progressed to racing. Burton sponsored her, and the USA snowboard team asked her to join. Putting the sponsorship on hold, she joined the team. The team represented the United States in many national and European events. She retired at twenty-five after six years on the racing circuit. When the resort opened three years ago, she took a job as the snowboard director.

The fact that she asked me to work for her at Elks Run was all it took for me to sign on. I learned quite a lot from Cathy about racing and teaching methods that I couldn't read in any book or get from a class.

"Yes, but I couldn't think of staying home and dreaming about all those beginning students who couldn't get down this hill without me. Besides, who would you give those students to?" I said.

"You're right. Welcome back, it's good to see you," she said.

"You too," I said as we gave each other a hug. "How are Steve and Justin?" Cathy's husband was a carpenter with his own contracting business, and Justin was her two-year-old son.

"Is Justin ready to start snowboarding?" I asked.

"Another year or two, he'll be ready. By the way, how's Stanley?" she asked.

"Oh, he's fine. As usual, he licks you to death." I was hoping she would not ask me about Debbie.

"Please, bring him by the lockers so I can say hello," she said.

"You bet. I didn't get a chance to tell you, but I'm taking over the maintenance of the resort's computers."

"Is that the proposal you submitted to the resort last summer?" she asked.

"Yep, that's it. I just want to say that if my resort pager or iPhone starts vibrating, I may have to take care of the issue."

"That isn't a problem. Just give me a call on the radio. I'll get someone else to take over the class for you," she added.

Cathy made a radio call to the ski school office and heard that a number of new, half-pipe and snow park students were coming to the assembly area. Since there were no intermediate or advanced snowboard students, Cathy divided the twelve students, both adults and teenagers, between three snowboard instructors. As we raised our hands, she told the students to report to us. The half-pipe and snow park students went with the younger instructors. They loved to do freestyle tricks and jumps.

A few years ago at another resort, I was learning to ride the pipe and make huge jumps. I was getting the hang of it until I went too high on a jump, tried to grab the bottom of my board, and lost sight of the ground. I landed on my wrist and fractured it. I couldn't live down that move with all the other instructors, and I returned to what I love to do. I wanted to perfect the "carved" turn and liked to work on my NASTAR racing. In little ways, I taught that controlling position on a snowboard is important. Was I a perfectionist? Probably, but I like to be called a "learning perfectionist."

"Mike, since I know you really love kids, I gave you four adults," Cathy said.

"Thanks, Cathy. You're so kind."

"I'll call you by radio and let you know if there are any students for the one o'clock class. If not, you're free for the day."

"That's fine with me." I picked up my board and headed for my four students. There were two guys and two women. Let the games begin.

# Chapter 11

Instructors needed to memorize the first names of the students. I remembered the names of other instructors by the way they skied or boarded; I memorized students by face association. It was a little bizarre. Bill had a big nose. His nose looked like a beak. Bill was a bird with a big beak. Mike had a large forehead that hiked above his eyes, so Mike is hiker. Mary has hair coming out of her hat, so Mary is a hairy ape. Putting it all together, I have a bird with a beak next to a hiker who meets a hairy ape. Okay, so it doesn't sound right, but it works for me. Diane looked a little like Debbie except for being a little smaller with flaming red hair and a tan completion. *I better not call her Debbie.*

It was a good mix. They were all snow skiers who wanted to learn to snowboard. I liked their attitudes. As adults, we're afraid to travel out of our comfort zones, and learning to snowboard will definitely take you out of that zone. Kids aren't embarrassed to fall and think it is fun to fall because they're closer to the ground. The trick to snowboarding is learning to fall correctly and having fun.

I checked to make sure everyone was hydrated. Today, almost everyone carried a CamelBak water system. It's a light backpack that you fill with water with an insulated long tube to suck the water from. Whether you are skiing or enjoying other outdoor activities in the mountains, hydration is important. It's not alcohol, the preferred Après ski beverage of choice.

I went over what they can expect from this level-one lesson. I talked about different types of snowboards and equipment including helmets. Hopefully, we can take the beginners chairlift and snowboard down the hill.

The principles of skiing and snowboarding are related. Each sport involves balancing, rotary, edge-control, and pressure-control movements. However, each sport applies it a little differently, depending on what you do on the slope. As a beginner, you concentrate on each movement. However, when you get to advanced levels of this sport, it's a subconscious movement. It's awareness and muscle repetition. That's what makes this sport so exciting. To see a beginning student take a morning lesson and apply the principles in the afternoon makes every instructor feel good.

We started by determining if everyone had the correct foot forward. I ride with my left foot forward, so I'm a regular-foot rider. If your right foot is forward, then you are considered a goofy-foot rider. How do you tell? You ask the student to walk forward to you. If he steps off on the left foot, then he's regular, and vice versa. It's not very scientific. Usually, the skier goes to a rental shop in town or at the resort, and they figure it out for him. However, sometimes, they're wrong.

During the lesson, I can tell whether the student needs to go back to the shop to get the bindings changed. They can pick up another class and start over. If I'm giving a private lesson, I'll change the bindings myself with a miniature ratchet wrench. As far as I know, everyone who snowboards carries this little handy tool to tweak bindings. I showed them a neutral stance. This is critical in snowboarding. You want to have a stance that puts your body directly over the board. You don't want to lean too far forward or backward on the board. If you're too forward on the board, you'll fall forward and do a face plant. You'll do a butt plant if you're too backward. Either way, it's a bone-jarring experience.

We started by doing straight-line glide and skate with one foot buckled in the binding and the safety strap attached to that leg. That safety line prevents a runaway board. With the other foot, we pushed off the snow to start the glide. The purpose of this exercise was to get the feeling of the board on the snow and to try to balance on top of it. Next, we progressed to side slipping with the board on a gentle slope, looking up and down the slope with one foot still in the binding and the unbuckled foot next to it. We tried to flatten the board to slide down the slope and then quickly get up on the edge to stop the slide. Leaving one foot out of the binding helps new snowboarders with balance.

I looked for balance, other movements, and the all-important neutral stance. Anyone without a neutral stance will have difficulty snowboarding. The reason I work out at the gym is that I need to be strong. I need my strength to pick up my students after they fall. When you fall with a pair of skis, it isn't that difficult to get up. You can use your poles to help. Snowboards are a little different. Literally, you have two feet locked on a board. Unless you are agile and have middle body strength, you'll need to unbuckle the bindings and get your feet out.

Heck, I have seen snowboarders in some precarious positions on the slopes. Having your head pointed down the slope isn't safe for a snowboarder or others on the slope. The motto is safety first. The skier safety code is covered in every lesson given and is posted at the ticket booths and other conspicuous places on the mountain. Just like driving, you have to follow the rules. Skiing is safe when you follow the rules and learn the skills.

I began by showing everyone how to get up on a snowboard and helped those who needed a little assistance. The guys take a little more finesse; Mary and Diane were like feathers. Diane was the lightest, and her smile was radiant. As she gave me her two hands and I pulled her up, her hair brushed against my face. I smelled the fragrance of sunflowers.

I shifted my thoughts back to the class and let go of her hands. I had everyone climb up a gentle slope. I showed them how to glide down the slope with the unbuckled foot behind the buckled forward foot. Everyone did well, and no one fell. That's when the fun began.

As they buckled their feet in both bindings, I checked everyone for proper fittings. I demonstrated how to sideslip facing down and up the hill. You're literally balanced on the edge of your board, and then you flatten it. You slide down the slope because you flatten the board on the snow, and you stop the slide by getting up on the edge again. For anyone new to this sport, it's a scary moment.

I took each one down the slope, doing a sideslip where I faced them up or down the hill on my board. If they needed my help, I told everyone to give me their hands for balance.

After a few trips down the slope, everyone was doing well and cheering for each other.

Diane seemed to be having a lot of fun with the lesson.

I asked them if anyone knows what a "fall-line" is in skiing. "If I were to take my snowboard to the top of the slope and let it go, it'd travel to the bottom of the slope, taking the shortest distance or in a straight line. We project our bodies over this line to uplift or lighten the board off the snow so we can turn and travel downhill. Then, we come back to a neutral position to control our direction. It's the same for skiers and snowboarders. Your next big hurdle is to ride the chairlift."

# Chapter 12

Before the start of every ski season, I try to see a Warren Miller film at the theater. It gets everyone psyched. Everyone is clapping, cheering, and wanting to ski and board in some the most beautiful places in the world. The funniest part of his films is when he shows how some beginning chair and rope lift riders attempt to make it up and out of the these lifts. Some of the film clips are old, but the laughs and cheers are contagious.

Well, with some instruction and humor, I try to cover the correct way. I know that riding a chairlift for the first time is a new skill, and I'm prepared to have a number of skiers sprawled in many directions as they plow into each other. It helps to show the proper way with the mock beginner's chair. Everyone seems to understand the principle of having either the left or right foot in the binding and gliding off the lift with the other foot on the board in the back of the one in the bindings. "Who said that you don't have to be coordinated in this sport?"

Since there were four students, the pairing off was easy. With the students behind my chair, they have their rear feet out of the bindings for push and balance. Diane and Mary were talking to each other, and Diane looked at me with a big smile. *Wow, she has a great smile.*

It was the time of reckoning, as we instructors liked to say among ourselves. *How well did I teach this concept, who listened, and who has balance?* With twenty feet to go, I signaled the lift operator to bring the chairlift to a snail's pace and put up two fingers to indicate that there were two chairs of students behind me. Reaching the top, I signaled the lift operator to really slow the lift down. I glided off to the side and quickly unbuckled my bindings.

Sticking my board in the snow to the right of the oncoming chair with Mary and Diane, I shouted, "Let the chair seat push you forward. Keep your free foot behind your front foot. Look ahead—not at your feet!"

Mary and Diane glided nicely; Diane went straight, and Mary went to the right.

I turned back to see Bill and Mike stand on their boards and attempt to get balance. Before I could shout out any instruction or encouragement, Mike went left and Bill went right. Unfortunately, the ends of their boards crossed on top of each other, and they fell with the lift chair just missing their heads. Quickly, I tried to move them out of the way of other skiers, but two other skiers came off the chair and headed directly at us, taking us down as if they were making a split spare in bowling. The lift operator stopped the lift and helped me unscramble the mess. After checking to make sure everyone was all right and gathering all the equipment, I took everyone over to the side, far away from the chairlift. I couldn't wait for the next time we take this lift.

After we talked about what happened, Bill and Mike profusely apologized for falling.

I told them that they'd do better the next time around. Looking at my watch, I saw that we had another thirty minutes left. I talked about our next great adventure. "We'll try to sideslip down a gentle slope, facing uphill and downhill. It sounds easier, but again it takes balance, edging, and complete control of your body position."

I moved to a small area off to the side of the slope and demonstrated the move, first facing uphill with my hands out in front of me for balance. Giving Mike and Bill a little time to catch their breath, I let Mary start facing uphill or in snowboard jargon "toe side."

She did well, and I took her hands in front of her while on my board. I slipped out of one binding and asked Mike to come down. He did well, but I noticed he grabbed my hands a little tighter than Mary did. Since Bob was ready to go, I watched him nervously sideslip. I asked him to look uphill over my shoulder and not at his board. Before I got a chance to get in front of Diane, she started and did a great job coming down. I was disappointed because I wanted to help her.

We did the same maneuver facing downhill or "heel side," and Mary was the first casualty. When I let go of her hands and moved to the side, she did a face plant on the snow, but she was all right. I picked her up and held her hands, and she finished fine.

Mike and Bill did well with a little handholding.

Diane had a little difficulty with the sideslip. I asked her to stop. Looking into her brown eyes, I said, "Diane, you need to be loose. So, take a breath and let it out slowly. You need to let your body be loose and not tight, okay?"

She gave me a big smile and a laugh. She finished the next twenty feet without a problem.

I said, "We're almost down to the point where we take the chairlift to the top of the beginner's slope. The chairlift is traveling over us."

I looked up and saw adults with trepidation and kids with smiles looking down at us. I asked everyone to meet me to the right of the chairlift after traversing down the slope on his or her toe side and heel side with a stop in between each maneuver. I showed them what it should look like twice. "There's no rush," I said. "Just make it good."

Mary started out first and did very well on both maneuvers.

Bill and Mike flipped a coin for who would go next. Mike lost and caught an edge on the toe side, but he kept his balance and finished well.

Bill needed to stop in the middle of both maneuvers, but he didn't fall. He finished with cheers from all of us.

Diane had good balance, edging, and stance. She finished with a big smile, and we all give her a hand.

I said, "I like what I see. If you continue with this sport, you can do very well."

In finishing the lesson, I went over what we had accomplished and what each of them needed to work on to take the next level class. "You took on a new challenge, and you did very well. Ride safe—and have fun."

As I picked up my board and headed back to the lockers, Diane came up behind me, tapped me on my shoulder, and thanked me for a great lesson.

I said, "The pleasure was all mine. You were a great student. I've never seen anyone with such a radiant smile."

Smiling again, she thanked me for the compliment. She picked up her board and walked back toward the main lodge.

I headed back to the lockers.

# Chapter 13

Locking my board in the rack, I headed over to the refrigerator to grab my lunch. Gus had already eaten his. I sat down to enjoy the roast beef sandwich that Ginny made. In a separate baggie, there were two kosher dill pickles. *This is going to taste wonderful.*

Cathy sat down across from me and asked me how my class had gone.

"It went well. I saw you off to the side."

"I apologize. One of your students is Joe Bunn's daughter."

"Don't tell me. Was it Diane?"

"Yes," she said. "From what I saw on the slope, I think she did well."

"Yes, she did very well. Is Diane working for Jean Sknosky in marketing?" I asked.

"Yes, she has been there for about a year now. I'll see you in the morning. You're next on my list for an advanced snowboard class. Also, Diane isn't dating anyone," she added with a smile.

*Didn't I say that there were very few secrets among instructors?*

After eating a great lunch and hydrating with a bottle of water, I gave Ginny a call on my cell phone.

"Hi, Mary. How's Stanley doing?"

"He's doing great. Ginny took a walk to the post office, and Stanley went with her. By the way, Ron said it was busy for him. Are you busy?"

"Yes, I had a class this morning, and I'm finished for today. I need to do some computer work here, but I should be able to pick up Stanley at the usual time this evening. If something comes up, I'll call."

"I'll pass that on to Ginny."

"Thanks. And have a good day."

Ron and Ginny were so lucky to have a great person working for them.

After getting dressed, I bumped into John Swan. I liked John because he was a good instructor and an all-around nice guy. He also took time out to teach me some half-pipe techniques that I wouldn't have learned any other way.

"Hey, Mike. A bunch of us are getting together at TT's later this afternoon. Interested?"

"John, that sounds good. I can't stay too late. I need to pick up Stanley at Gus's."

"Too bad you can't bring him along," he said with a smile.

"John, I can't afford to get chewed out by Bob again," I added with a smile.

TT's was the resort's bar and grill, which opened for lunch and closed at one in the morning. I once sneaked Stanley in with a crowd of us and proceeded to take a back table. We were all having a great time until Stanley started barking and baying. I think someone got on the floor and started playing with him.

Bob didn't like dogs in the bar and threw us all out. He told the ski school director, and the rest is history.

It took me about five minutes to reach the computer room. Logging into the database and management console, a screen came up. It showed me the health condition of both databases, including how much space was being used and if the data was being sent over to the backup database without any problems. The most important information was the alerts I set up on it. I wanted to make sure that they were still in effect and working. The alert was important because I didn't want the databases to have any issues for the daily resort activity and department reporting. It would also let me know if the resort lost power or the databases crashed.

The resort generators had a few seconds of lag time before full power was restored. When power was restored, the databases would automatically restart based upon the code I wrote. But, if they didn't start, I'd need to start them manually. The alerts told me whether I needed to start them manually by sending an e-mail or a thirty-character text message.

One area that I'm unsure of was how much database file space I would need for the daily lift operations. There was a schedule for all lift maintenance, wire tensions, speeds, temperature of the bottom and top lift structures, and even movement of the towers throughout the day in real-time.

Looking at my notes from the first management meeting, I wrote down that Brian Jones was using a new software program, which was capable in capturing all this information. He needed to graph it on a two-day interval for two weeks. After two weeks, he was going to delete it and keep a hard copy. From experience, I knew that capturing and graphing this information on a screen or a spreadsheet involved using the database's spatial graphic package and took a lot of space. I had ample space for now, but I needed to check it tomorrow and the next day. Otherwise, everything looked good.

Another responsibility was the two e-mail servers. If the resort could not send or receive e-mails, all hell would break loose. I needed to make sure that they were up and running and that there was enough space on them. Again, redundancy is beautiful, but space is at a premium. When the e-mails reached a certain capacity, it went to a backup drive for storage. This concept of storage has been around since the 1970s when data and backups were written to a tape drive; now hard drives or flash drives were used. When the resort business slowed down in the summer, it wrote over that drive with new e-mails.

Speaking of tape drives, I have a cassette record player relic with big buttons for record, forward, reverse, and play with an earplug jack. I couldn't part with it. As long as I can buy the cassettes somewhere on the internet, I liked using it.

"Why buy the album or song when you can borrow it from the local library and record it," Debbie used to say. "You can use that money to buy a latte." I wondered how she was doing.

I left the computer room, walked to my truck, and looked at the closed lifts. The ski patrol began sweeping all the trails from the top of the mountain to the bottom for any injured or lost skiers. I remembered working ski patrol on the East Coast and finding a skier who had lost a ski and started the long walk down the mountain. With the lifts closed, there weren't any skiers coming down the slope to help him. I stopped, and he got a nice ride down the mountain on the toboggan. Ski patrollers play a vital role on the mountain as does everyone else who is part of the resort mountain team.

Safety is paramount, and it's taken seriously.

# Chapter 14

TT's is about a quarter mile from the main lodge. It was a nice walk, but since it had begun to snow, I drove. Walking from the parking lot to TT's, I passed through the main promenade of the resort entrance. I passed a number of closed top-line clothing and eating shops.

TT's was crowded with most of the resort employees. The bar was right in the middle of the place. Usually, the instructors gathered at the far end of the bar.

John Swan waved, and Ron was sitting next to him. I waved to them, saying hello to a few patrollers and lift operators along the way. Finally, I reached John and Ron.

"Hey, Mike. Good to see that you made it," John said.

"How many times do I have to tell you that you need to pay attention to the company you keep," I said with a laugh. "Since you two have been waiting for me, I'm going to buy the next round. A Coors light for me," I said to the bartender. "Ron, you seemed real busy today—or was that my imagination."

"No, I was busy, and it felt good. Maybe, this season will be good one, especially when we are able to use the new back bowl."

"John, what do you think about the new gondola and the back bowl?" I asked.

"I hope it'll bring the skiers that the resort promised, but I heard that PineTree is mobilizing people to prevent the lift from opening."

"John, I know they're a little sore that the Forest Service gave the Elks Run the lift permit, but there were debates in town hall meetings among the resort, townspeople, the Forest Service, and even some local congressmen. Surely, it was fair. Wasn't it?" I asked.

"I know there were numerous meetings that we business owners held in town about the advantages and disadvantages of this lift and the expansion of the condominium in the resort and the advantages won," Ron added.

"As you guys know, I'm in my last year at UC, majoring in environmental studies. I wrote a paper on the environmental impact these types of expansions have on our wilderness, especially in Colorado. It just so happens that I know a couple of the local PineTree people. They answered my questions on these issues, including the Elks Run expansions. Their feeling is that it wasn't so fair," he said.

"John, what would you expect? I understand that we need to control growth because God knows we haven't done a good job, but Colorado depends on the ski season and all the other seasons because a great percentage of our economy comes from tourism," I said.

John said, "Listen, you both have open minds on many issues, and I like bouncing my thoughts off you. I would love for one or both of you to attend an open discussion with the PineTree organization at the Elks Center in a few weeks about the environmental issues affecting Colorado today. In addition, I can introduce you to the members I interviewed for my paper," he said.

"It all depends on the date and time," Ron said.

"I agree that taking care of our environment has to be a high priority, but to obtain that environmental goal is not, let's say, putting their best foot forward with some of their illegal activities we hear and read in the media. Also, working as a consultant for the resort would make me think twice before I attend any meeting with this group," I said.

"Fair enough," John answered.

"Speaking of tourism and all that, I need to tour the men's room. I'll be right back; if not, I'll buy the next round," I said.

"We'll hold you to it," Ron said.

As I made my way to the men's room, I felt a tap on my shoulder.

I turned around, and Diane Bunn said, "Hi, Mike. Could I buy you and your friends a drink?"

"Diane, how come you didn't tell me that you and Diane Bunn are one and the same?" I asked.

"Oh, Mike. I didn't think it would be fair to you or me. I think I couldn't be as 'loose' as you wanted me to be," she said with her wonderful smile. She wore tight jeans, boots, and a yellow pullover sweater that made her pulled-back red hair look as though it was on fire.

"Diane, if it wasn't for that enchanting smile of yours, which could melt the ice in an ice machine, I would have to agree," I said. "I would love to take you up on the drink and so would my friends, but I need to leave in the next fifteen minutes or so."

"Oh, a hot date?" she asked with a sad face.

"Yes, I've to pick up Stanley."

"Oh, I didn't think you were that type of guy—not that it would matter to me."

"Oh, no, Stanley is my dog. He's staying with Ron's wife at their shop. Ron is sitting with me at the bar. He's the one with the big mustache. And that's John Swan, another excellent snowboard instructor."

"Oh, Mike. I know about Stanley because Jean has already told me about him and how wonderful he is. I'm just kidding, and I would like to meet him sometime," she said with a chuckle.

"I would like to take you up on that offer and take the next step in my snowboard career. Would you be interested in teaching me a level two as a private lesson?" she asked.

"Well, sure. That would be great, and I think you'll do well," I said.

"What would be a good time for you?" she asked.

"Since you probably know that I'm the computer consultant at the resort, I like doing my classes in the morning. If need be, I can stop by the computer room right after lunch."

"Yes, my dad did say that you are taking care of the resort computers. Mornings would be fine, but how can we coordinate a lesson?"

"I don't usually do this for everyone, but I don't have my cards with me. I'll write my home and cell phone number on this bar napkin. Just leave a message on either one, and I can call you back. Would that be okay?"

"I'm flattered to receive this bar token from you. This is great. I'll be looking forward to it," she said with a laugh and walked to a table of women on the other side of the bar.

I bought the next round for being late. They knew that I needed to solicit business whenever possible, especially when the business comes to you. I was thinking in that direction. *Maybe I'm flattered that a beautiful woman was flirting with me.* I needed to get on the road. I said, "I need to pick up Stanley. I'll probably see you both tomorrow."

"No problem," John said.

"Tell Ginny, I'll be home shortly after stopping at the market to pick up some things," Ron said.

"See you on the slopes," John added.

"Drive safely," I said and headed for the door. Stepping out into the crisp air, I looked up and saw the Big Dipper. *This air and climate is so great. Colorado is a great place to live.*

# Chapter 15

Leaving the resort, I glanced up and saw the distinct lights of the snow cats grooming the slopes. Many skiers take the hard work and skill of these workers for granted. When the resort closes for the day, their work begins. On those powerful and agile snow cats with special equipment, they smooth the rough slopes and ruts throughout the night. That's why all skiers want to be the first ones on the slopes. Being the first ones on the slope was one of our better work benefits.

Driving down from the resort was slow, but the road was plowed and sanded. I found an unusual parking spot in front of the shop and entered the front door.

Ginny waved.

Stanley didn't notice me because a good-looking teenage girl was petting him. He knew how to work the crowd. When he finally saw me, he charged at me. I got down on all fours to take the full charge. Basset hounds are one of the happiest hound breeds. You can be gone for fifteen minutes, and they will greet you as if you had been gone for days. It was the nature of the breed.

After reminding Ginny that Ron should be home shortly and thanking her for looking after Stanley, I went home.

Stanley must have had a busy day because he immediately fell asleep on the passenger seat. I needed to wake him when we got home. If he had been driving, I would be the one falling asleep. My lower back and legs were aching. *I guess that's the price of getting older, but I would never admit it to anyone. Well, maybe to Ron and no one else.*

I fed Stanley, checked the mail and messages, swallowed a few Ibuprofens with water, and took Stanley for a brief walk. I planned to eat my dinner while taking a nice Jacuzzi bath. *I may even fall asleep along the way, hopefully not in the tub. When the sun rises, Stanley will let me know about his need to eat and take a walk.*

While feeding Stanley his dinner, Cathy called.

"Hi, Cathy. Do you need someone to teach a beginner's class tonight?"

"Funny. I got a heads-up on the early morning classes tomorrow, and it looks as though I have enough instructors. I know you are tired from today, and you can rest up or do whatever you need to. Is that all right with you?"

"That's fine with me. Just because I am dragging my board doesn't mean I'm hurting," I said laughing.

"Can you take Diane Bunn for a lesson at eleven tomorrow. She asked for you."

"She asked if I would like to teach her a level 2 class about an hour ago. She works fast, if you need to know," I said with some amusement.

"You cannot trust those red-haired women. Now, are you going to teach her a class and give me a director's gold star, something that I'll cherish for a lifetime?"

"Sure. I can help you out," I said. "Say hello to Steve, and give Justin a hug from me."

"Sure, Mike. Thanks."

I walked to the kitchen, and the phone rang again.

"Stanley, it seems as though I'm the go-to guy tonight."

It's Debbie. How are you doing tonight?"

"Oh, fine." I was surprised to hear her voice.

"I just called to ask you about your first day back on the slopes."

"Oh, there's nothing like Ibuprofen and a warm bath to help those muscles that I didn't use all year. I had a beginner's class to start the season. Cathy always starts me out slowly," I said.

"How are Cathy, Steve, and little Justin?"

"Oh, fine. I think they may be thinking of having another baby. That is the impression I get from Cathy."

"That's great. Mike, I was wondering if you still get the free passes. Jessica and I would like to come up and ski on a weekday. Would that be all right?"

"Sure. If you can give me heads-up, I can leave the passes with Ginny," I said.

"No, that wouldn't be a problem with me if it's not with you? I would like to see Ginny," she added.

"That's not a problem for me. How's work?"

"I'm busy with a couple of defense cases. Just to get away from them, even for a day, would be great."

"I know how a day in the mountains would help," I said. "All those long hours."

"Hug Stanley for me, and be careful out there," she said.

"You too," I said and hung up the phone.

I remembered when we used to watch the reruns of a cop show on a cable channel in Virginia, and the sergeant always told his men to "be careful out there." We watched the program from our bed, eating popcorn and ice cream.

I ran to the bathroom to shut off the water and got into the tub. Stanley took his usual position on the bath mat. I turned on the Jacuzzi jets and closed my eyes.

It had been a long day for both of us.

# Chapter 16

Waking up at seven, Stanley's usual time, I managed to convince him to stay in his bed for another thirty minutes. Putting on my Hot Chill's thermals, jeans, and sweater, I took him for a walk to the mailbox. It had snowed another four inches, giving us about fifteen inches in a week.

At Elks Run, the base was about twenty inches; the top should be about thirty-five inches. I considered the snow a good omen for a great season. The sun was shining brightly, but it was hard to tell by the snow clouds in the sky. The mailbox was full of junk mail. *I should suggest to the homeowners association that they put a garbage can right at boxes. It could save all of us time from walking back with all this junk mail. However, I do carry it back because I use it to start the fireplace. Maybe, the other owners do the same.*

Before toasting a bagel, I fed Stanley his breakfast and turned on the TV. I was right about the possibility of snow. I missed my vocation. I should have taken meteorology as my major in school and become a weatherman. In the winter, it snowed a good 85 percent of the time in this part of the state. It's not hard to predict. The talk show host was talking about the promising ski season and the gondola. *Oh, that reminds me to either stop by or give Brian Jones a call about his lift data. It seems to be eating up database space at a very fast rate. I need to take a shower, take Stanley for another walk, and get ready to teach a snowboard lesson to a beautiful redhead with a great smile.*

Leaving a little earlier enabled me to stop at the Coffee Cup Café, get some coffee, and let Ginny know that I'd be leaving Stanley home today. It was getting close to the Thanksgiving, and we'd get a lot of business from kids off from school, others off from work, and visitors from around the globe. No one would guess that a number of our tourists were from the UK. In fact, I sometimes felt as though I should be ordering a cup of tea instead of coffee at the main lodge. However, they're fun guests and great tippers.

Driving up the pass to the resort, the area where the gondolas and other equipment had been unloaded, was empty. I had heard rumors that the gondolas would start for the checkout runs. *Since I'm going to stop by and speak to Brian Jones today, I think I'll ask him. It's amazing how just getting here thirty minutes earlier gets you a better employee parking space. I'm savoring this spot because I don't think I will see a spot like this ever again.*

After putting my lunch in the refrigerator, I saw Cathy. "I'll be back to give that lesson to Diane at eleven, okay?"

"I know you will," she said with a smile.

I smiled back and shook my head. *Diane is a beautiful single woman who happens to be the daughter of the resort president. Why do women think that men always have an ulterior motive? I guess we do.*

It took me about five minutes to get to the computer room. While waiting to log on to the database, I walked over to the other flat-screen monitor and logged into the e-mail servers to check them out. They come up quickly, and I typed in a cryptic status command. *Gee, the allocated space is filing up quickly. Okay, who's taking up all this space?*

Another cryptic command gives me Joe Bunn and Brian Jones. I can see Joe sending and receiving many e-mails, but Brian Jones isn't. *Unless he is sending that graphic information as attachments to his e-mails, one e-mail server is running out of space. I think I need to suggest that we limit the file size attachments that employees can send and receive. That's the correct way to approach this problem. Most e-mail administrators just set a limit on the file attachment sizes and plead ignorance when the complaints start coming in. Better yet, I can set the limit and leave for a vacation. Oh, those were the good old days. The save-my-job correct way is to move some of these e-mail address files off to the backup drive and send an e-mail to all employees to limit their attachment sizes. Then, they get an error message pop-up if it is exceeded. That way, employees can still access their old e-mails, and it does not hamper them from sending or receiving new mail. It's what we call user transparency. They don't need to know if there isn't any available space because we give them space without them knowing that we do. However, I'm curious to see if my theory of sending and receiving large attachments is correct. Opening Brian Jones's file, I see from a quick scan of his e-mail addresses that he is sending attachments and receiving e-mails from only two other e-mail addresses, Joe.Bunn@elksrunresort.com and Robert. Frost@skystream.com. Where have I seen that name? Yes, I know. Sky Stream is installing the new gondola lift.*

*There is a simple explanation for this amount of mail, and it's probably that the key people need to coordinate all this activity among them. Heck, the lift's opening day is not far away. I'm creating more space on this e-mail server by compressing the space. Since the creation of the Internet, the average person just doesn't know what goes on behind the scenes or how this all happens and the work it takes to keep it all going. With a simple mistake or miscalculation, no one can receive any e-mails. In the past, it was the mail carrier. Today, it is the e-mail administrator. Because my mom doesn't use e-mail, I like to take the time to send her a written letter. It allows me to see how I construct my letters and whether I can still write a sentence in a straight line. I would be embarrassed to say how many times I start the letter and then rip it up because my sentences start curving to the bottom of the paper and look illegible. I pride myself on writing on notepaper that isn't lined. I remember the old school copybooks in which I printed the letters of the alphabet. I wouldn't get credit if a letter drifted over the lines.*

I logged off the e-mail server and pushed the play button of my cassette player on Stanley's bed. Putting on the headphones, I listened to music while I looked and see if there were any issues with the database. I ran a few scripts that I had written in procedural language called SQL. This data access script language was based upon industry-accepted standards. The scripts comprise of SQL statements that allow me to access, update, and even delete the data that is stored in an object-relational Oracle database. It's written in English-like format, but there are certain a words or clauses that need to be used. These scripts give me a snapshot of how the database is performing, if there are any bottlenecks with users who connect to it, whether I need to add space or a data file to it, or if there are any network problems. It's important that I run them.

I run a few more scripts and see that everything is working fine for today. Tomorrow is another day. I logged off the databases and e-mail servers, shutting off the flat-screen monitors. Leaning back in my chair, I listened to the end of the song. *Well, it's time to have some fun.* I reached down and shut off the cassette player, took off my headphones, and headed out the door.

# Chapter 17

After running my ID badge through the employee clock and saying hello to a few instructors straggling in to take late teaching assignments, I headed out the door to meet Diane. The sky was crisp blue with a few clouds off to the north. A slight breeze from the west was dipping over the mountain. I looked at the thermometer clipped to my bib overalls; it was registering a pleasant forty-four degrees. There's a difference of about fifteen degrees from the base of the mountain to the top at 12,377 feet. *When the new lift opens, it will travel to 12,777 feet with unparalleled views.*

Diane was waiting at the Stairwell lift, which was for the beginner and intermediate runs. When she saw me, she started tapping her watch, rolling her eyes, and showing signs of disgust. As I approached, she said, "I'm not paying for an instructor that's late, and I'm demanding a refund."

"Your watch is fast because my watch said 11:00 on the dot," I said with a smile.

She smiled back and said, "You're safe. I won't tell anyone."

"Okay, let's take Stairwell and talk about what we'll cover today."

Since we both rode regular, we stepped into the soft bindings and strapped our left foot on the board, gliding on our boards by taking our right foot and pushing the board forward in a glide so we can put it behind our left foot. Stepping in front of the chairlift, we sat down and pulled the safety bar over our heads. We took a comfortable position by slightly picking up our boards with our left foot and putting them on the instep of our free feet. This was the most comfortable way of riding a lift and not letting the board dangle from the chair.

"So, what I'd like to cover with you today is linking the turns. In the first lesson, you learned to do a reverse traverse or a toe-side glide across the slope as you looked down the slope. Then, you did a hillside garland with a glide across the slope. That was when you looked up the slope. What I'll teach you today is to link both of these maneuvers across the fall line. Do you remember what the 'fall line' is in snowboarding?"

"I remember you saying that if I were to take my snowboard to the top of the slope and let it go, it would travel to the bottom of the slope in the shortest distance or in a straight line. That is the line that we project our bodies over to make our turns. It's the same for skiers and snowboarders."

"I'm speechless. How did you remember all that information? You must be brilliant in Trivial Pursuit. Even I couldn't remember that my first time."

"You would be surprised by what I'm capable of doing," she answered with a smile.

Before I could respond, it was time to put the safety bar up and get ready to glide off the lift. I put my mind back on the lesson. "Okay, Diane. I'll go straight, and you can go to the right."

We stood up on our boards, put our right foot behind the left one, and safely glided off.

"Great job, Diane," I said as she glided off to the right without failing. "Now, let's move over to the far side of the slope and buckle into our bindings. Make sure the safety strap is clipped around your front leg."

I asked her to sit facing downhill as we reviewed the first lesson. Then, we physically performed those same maneuvers on the slope. I was impressed that she did well, but I reminded her be more centered on her board and to distribute her weight equally over the board. Then, looking up the hill for any approaching skiers, I showed how I would start facing up the hill doing a toe-side edge with my body centered over the board in a relaxed position and my down-slope left hand pointing in the direction that I wanted to travel. About twenty feet from her, I flattened my board and let it take the fall line down the slope. As it pointed downhill, I applied heel edging as my entire body faced downhill. I gripped the slope with my heel edge and glided across the slope in the other direction with my up-slope left hand facing uphill. I skidded to a stop about ten feet below where she was watching me.

"Bravo. That looks so cool," she said with a big smile. "Can you do it again?"

"No, it's my time to rest. Now it's your turn," I answered with a sly grin.

"Rats. Just when I started to enjoy this sport," she said.

"Just remember to let your body stay loose," I added. Well, except for a shaky start and a little trouble with the fall-line toe-side turn to me, she did well.

As we practiced the turns down the hill, she got stronger. I saw the determination of someone who did not like to give up on a new challenge.

The hour went by quickly with two more runs down the hill. Finishing off the lesson, I reviewed what we'd covered and the areas that she needed to practice to develop these skills.

"Mike, when can I take the next level lesson?" she asked enthusiastically.

"Diane, you did well, but I think you'll need to practice these turns so that you can automatically perform them before you move to the next level," I said.

"Okay, I guess you're right. Since I cannot take a level three until I practice a little more, I want to take you out for lunch. How about we meet at lodge for a late lunch, if that's all right with your schedule?"

I was a little stunned by her invitation. It's not that I didn't want to have lunch with a beautiful, outgoing, and very bright woman who I was attracted to, but maybe I just wanted to be by myself. "I would like to, but I have a number of things to do. I wonder if I can take a rain check on it," I said.

"Sure, Mike. However, if you have a change of plans, I'll be there at three," she said disappointedly.

I watched her walk toward the main lodge and figured I should have said yes.

# Chapter 18

I walked into the locker room, locked up my board, and dressed. It was 12:30. I grabbed my lunch from the refrigerator and was headed toward the computer room until I saw Ron sitting down eating his lunch. "Ron, mind if I join you? Without Stanley, it does get a little lonely eating in the computer."

"Hey, take a seat Mike. I'm finished for the morning. I got a return lesson from yesterday at two and need to get some fuel," he answered.

I got a soft drink from the vending machine, sat down, and picked up the employee newsletter. On the front page, I saw a picture of Joe Bunn and Brian Jones next to a gondola. The article explained how they were excited about the new lift and gave some statistics about how many skiers it will carry to the top of Buffalo Mountain. The testing of the lift would be an ongoing process, and it may be running throughout the day and night. In addition, there may be employees chosen to ride the lift and complete a questionnaire about the experience.

"Mike, don't tell me you're reading the resort newspaper?"

"Ron, I'm reading to see when we're going to get that pay increase we were promised."

"I heard that it is retroactive, beginning with this paycheck."

"Great! I was also reading about the gondola lift and they will let some employees test the lift. Want to go, buddy?"

"I wouldn't mind. Just to see the back bowl would be a trip. Besides, since you're teaching Diane Bunn to board, I think you can ask Joe Bunn or Brian Jones if we can go."

"Sure, I'll do it," I said.

I looked around the locker room, and no one was around. "Seriously, Ron. I've got a question to ask you. I gave Diane two snowboard lessons, and she has done great. With practice, I think she can become a good boarder. However, after today's lesson, she asked me if I wanted to have lunch with her. I took a rain check. One part of me wanted to go, and the other said no. I felt a little guilty and wondered what would her father—and everyone else around this resort—would say."

"I can't entirely empathize with you, but I'll give it a try. The facts are that you are divorced. Just as you're trying to develop your business, you need to try to broaden your social life. Asking you to lunch doesn't mean anything. Maybe she wants you to be her friend. Debbie was exceptionally bright and a fine person, but Debbie isn't here, and you are. Make the most of it. Ginny and I wish the best for you and Debbie. I hope I answered your question—even though it may have been a little long."

"Thanks, buddy."

We talked about getting together and doing some runs together. I needed to get on my skis so I wouldn't forget how to ski, and I liked to ski with Ron. However, he never wanted to put on snowboard, even when I dared him. He thought that it was not natural to have his feet strapped to a board.

We agreed to get to work earlier and take a run down from the top in the next couple of days. We used to do race at least once a week to see who was faster. A good skier always beats a good boarder. There's less resistance with two skis. I'm not including some of those wide or fat skis you see on the slopes today. Unless Ron stops in a mogul or takes air on a bump, I usually end up buying a round or two for him at TT's. It gets expensive.

I said good-bye and headed for the computer room. I checked out the database and the e-mail servers, and everything looked well. My analysis from a few days ago was right on, and that was a relief. It was a little before three. I thought about what Ron said and headed for the main lodge.

It might be fun to find out a little more about Diane because she certainly knows a little bit about me.

# Chapter 19

Heavenly Lodge, located at the Village in Elks Run, was busy with activity. The main lodge was a huge log cabin. I remembered seeing it with Ron and the layout of the lifts and trails when it was being built. The Appalachian square logs had tongue and grooves cut on the top to make up the major exterior of the lodge.

They fit on top of each other, using a butt and pass technique. This type of log home construction was used in this area over a hundred years ago. We learned this and a lot more when one of the supervisors took us for a tour. I took pride in knowing a little of this and that, but building log homes wasn't one of them.

The same type of artisanship was reflected with the inside décor—in the hand-carved stairs and banisters leading to the large observation deck, the beautifully carved bar with matching stools and wide-planked wood floors, and the individual conversation areas fitted with comfortable chairs, ottomans, sofas, and lamps.

At Elks Run, I felt as though I was entering the main lodge in a European resort. Money wasn't a problem building this resort. On the way to the restaurant, I passed a number of Western-themed oil paintings by Colorado painters.

I stopped to admire a painting that showed the pastoral fields of wildflowers of Crested Butte when I felt a tap on my shoulder.

"Hi, Mike. I hope you came for lunch," Diane said.

"Oh, hi, Diane. Yes, and I thought it was you because of how you tapped me on the shoulder," I said.

"Oh, I'm sorry. I do have a bad habit. I just arrived, and I'm happy that you came. Let's take a seat and order lunch. I'm starving," she said.

"Sure, let's do it." We selected a table with a view of the ski lift. At its passenger pickup point, there was a new gondola. As we sat down, Diane said, "Doesn't the lift look great? I guess I'll need to work on turning so I can take it to the top and enjoy the back bowl"

"Yes, it certainly does. And the best part is that it'll be able to be enjoyed all year round," I said.

"Are you telling me that everything I learned from you doesn't guarantee me a chance of taking the lift this winter?" she asked with a slight grin.

"Oh, I didn't mean it that way, but practicing does help," I answered.

"I know I need to work on a lot of things. Did you have any problems learning snowboarding, or am I the only klutz?"

"No. I had similar problems, but I had these problems on the East Coast where failing on icy snow wasn't something you wanted to do more than a couple times. To be honest, since I board most of the time, it could take me some time to adjust to skis," I said.

"Thanks for the reassurance," she said.

Diane ordered a sirloin burger with sautéed onions and fries; since I already had already eaten, I had a coffee with chocolate cake.

Out of the blue, Diane hit me with a solid right. "Mike, I don't want you to think I'm trying to probe into your personal life, but I hear that you recently got divorced. I don't want to compound your issues. Please tell me if I'm out of bounds, and I'll completely understand," she said with a look of concern.

"Diane, I appreciate your sensitivity, but it's not a total secret, as you probably know, when you work at a ski resort," I answered with a slight grin.

"I guess you're right," she answered as our food arrived.

As we started eating, I thought I needed to change the conversation. "I read in the employee newsletter that you attended an Ivy League college on the East Coast. As you probably guessed from my accent, I'm from Upstate New York State. I graduated from St. John's University in Queens, New York. What school did you attend?"

"I graduated from Columbia University with a degree in marketing, and I joined Western Ventures right out of college. At the time, my dad was senior VP of resort operations, but I started at the bottom and learned what role marketing plays in the service industry. When the resort was ready to open and Dad was promoted to CEO, my mom asked if I would like to come back to the States. I had been working as an assistant director of marketing at a Western Ventures resort in Montreux, Switzerland. It was a few miles east of Lake Geneva. I did miss my folks and Colorado. We have a condominium in Vail, and I have many fond memories of Vail."

"It seems to me that seeing your parents, living in Colorado, and marketing this resort would be an incentive to come to this resort, but I have the impression that there was something else that made that decision easier for you."

"Mike, you're very perceptive—or you can read people very well," she answered.

I did not know what to say and waited for her to continue.

"I was seriously involved with a person that my parents only met once when they visited me last year. He was in charge of condominium developing for the resort in Switzerland. I thought it would be a great opportunity if he came with me to this resort, but he said that he couldn't because he was leaving Western Ventures to go into business for himself. I would have probably stayed in Switzerland with him, but he said that he was also going to marry the woman he was dating before he met me."

"Ouch. Sorry to hear that, but I have been told that it must be for the best. That's what my mom said to me when Debbie and I divorced. I'm still trying to figure that out."

"Wow. I must get back to work, and I'm probably holding you up also," she said as she looked at her watch. "I'm sorry that I bored you and that you didn't get a chance to say a word."

"You didn't bore me, and I liked your honesty."

"I like that fact that you listen. Maybe we can talk again at when we're not rushed?"

"That would be great. Can I call you about a time and date?"

"Oh, that would great," she said.

"Thanks for the lunch. Have a good rest of the day," I said.

"You too. And say hello to Stanley for me."

*She is beautiful, diligent in her work, open to new adventures, and knows the direction she wants to go. She got my attention. I'm older and wiser, and I know that first impressions are sometimes misleading. I need to thank Debbie for being a good listener and Ron for his advice.*

# Chapter 20

When I got home, Stanley was one happy basset hound. We spent five minutes on the floor just roughhousing with each other. If you don't think a fifty-five-pound dog with small legs can stop you in your tracks as you try to run away from him as he latches onto one of your ankles, you don't know how much fun you are missing.

After missing each other for a good part of the day, it was time for a walk. The snow was piling up on the sides of the road, and walking on the shoulders of the main road wasn't a possibility. In Leadville, the snow piled up every winter. I would have to inch my way through a stop sign to see the oncoming traffic because the snow was piled at least twelve feet high on the sides of the road. It was intimidating for those who weren't use to driving in it. However, for the natives, it was everyday life.

Since there hardly any traffic, Stanley and I walked on the road. The air was crisp, and the stars were brilliant. I think one of the great joys in life is having the opportunity to look up in the sky and marvel at the moon and stars. When I was young, my friends and I would try to explain to each other what was the moon made of and who lived on it. Now, we know what the moon is and that no one lives on it yet, but I'm still in awe when I see a full moon; especially, on a cold crisp night.

Stanley and I settled down to a great dinner, and I checked my phone messages. Larson's Salvage Company left a message about pushing our meeting to ten. *What? I have a meeting tomorrow? I forgot all about that meeting.* On my calendar, there was a nine o'clock meeting with them. I needed to talk about helping them manage their servers and desktop computers. *Boy, I need to discipline myself and set alerts in my iPhone calendar. I can't let this happen.*

Debbie always reminded me in the morning and evening. I sometimes got annoyed when she did, but I needed that discipline now. I called Cathy and left a message that I wouldn't be in tomorrow. When an instructor doesn't show up for work, it gives someone else a chance to earn a little income. Having a bunch of instructors hanging out for a class was awkward for Cathy because she needed to decide who worked and who didn't. I just made it easier for her.

There were days when a few of us just didn't want to work and just wanted to have fun shredding all over the mountain. We also liked cutting in front of everyone on the lifts and getting more runs. On other days, we worked on skills that we wanted to sharpen or that were required for level. The days we showed up for lineup counted as days worked—whether we worked, trained, or had fun.

After my meeting, I would spend some quality time with Stanley, catch up with the mail, and work out at the gym. I sat back and thought about the lunch with Diane. I guess our society teaches us to compare one brand to another, one experience to another, and one person to another. It would be foolish to compare Debbie to Diane, but it was my nature to take on a challenge, be honest, and respect others. I learned that from my folks.

Since Ron and I worked a very busy Thanksgiving Day, Ginny asked Mary to close the shop while she prepared the dinner. Stanley and I enjoy a wonderful feast at their place. I never thought about what it would feel like to not spend holidays with Debbie. We always shared our holidays with friends and sometimes had Ron and Ginny down to our place in Denver.

As I sat down with Ron and Ginny, I thought about Debbie. It was hard to push her out of my mind. I compare it to a day of fly-fishing on the Arkansas River. I made a perfect cast just behind a log eddy in one of the best areas for a fish waiting to strike a fly. The fish strikes and I am just a tad slow to snag it. I felt the strike and lost it. If I let it nag me, I wouldn't have a good day. I might as well pack up my gear and leave.

That same feeling came to mind when I thought about Debbie. *I've lost control of the situation. If I let it bother me throughout the day, the day will be worthless. I just can't let that happen today or any other day. So many other holidays, birthdays, and anniversaries will come and go. I have to make the most of every day. I have Stanley and good friends, but I wonder if Debbie feels the same way.*

# Chapter 21

T he days between Thanksgiving and New Year's were very busy. Ron and I agreed that the number of people skiing was more than in the past three years. Our feelings were right on line when I checked the tickets purchased from a query on the database. It was about 10 percent higher than last year's numbers. It was a combination of many things. We had an abundance of great snow, fast lift service, excellent food, ski programs for kids and adults, and condominium sales.

The marketing was better than at any other resort in the state. Jean and Diane were doing everything short of walking on water to get the word out. I didn't see Diane as much as I had before the holidays. We talked on the phone a few times and had an unofficial date on the slope. That was okay. Our conversations had passed the point of explaining our past failures, and we were looking forward to making the most of the present.

Ron had been right about suggesting lunch with Diane. At that time in my life, I never thought that I could ever feel comfortable talking to anyone besides Debbie. I felt a little helpless. I had a different perspective on divorce. I was so lucky to have down-to-earth friends like Ron and Ginny. I enjoyed hanging out with Stanley. He and I had become an item, so to speak, at the resort.

When Debbie and I talked on the phone, she always asked about Stanley. Being the low person on the totem pole, she struggled through court cases, trying to wrap them up before the holidays. However, I knew that she wasn't that happy working long hours. Possibly, over the holidays, she and Jessica would come up and ski at the resort. It had been postponed a number of times, but my invitation for lift tickets still stood.

I had sent a gift to my mom to beat the last-minute mailers. She loved to read, and I picked up her favorite author in large print because age had its limitations. However, she was physically healthy and spunky to boot. It must have been all her wild friends. Her closest friend was ninety and had battled a number of personal tragedies, including cancer, and still had time to bowl in a league. She averaged 120; I don't think I could bowl a hundred. I was so happy for her.

After picking up Stanley's scattered toys and going through the mail, the phone rang.

"Did I get you at a bad time?" Diane asked. "I can call back later."

"No, you don't have to. I was just starting to read the mail."

"Did you get the invitation my dad sent out to the staff for a New Year's party at their home?"

I looked through the pile and found the letter addressed to me from the resort. I tore it open while I wedged the phone between my shoulder and ear. It was about two weeks away and was not formal. That's good. "Yes. I just read it, and I am planning to go."

"Oh, that's great. I'm glad that you'll be there," she said enthusiastically. "Mike, can I ask a favor of you?"

"Teach you to do bumps on a snowboard?" I answered jokingly.

"Yeah, in my dreams. I know you have a pickup, and I was hoping that you could help me pick out a Christmas tree and bring it to my place so I can decorate it. If you feel uncomfortable about it, I completely understand."

I really didn't know what to say. Even married to Debbie, I didn't like decorating the tree because of all the intricate decorations. I didn't have the patience. I just set up the tree, helped with the lights, and let her do the artistic stuff. "Diane, to be honest, I like to pick out a tree and set it up, but I'm not really good at hanging decorations."

"That's all right. I can decorate it, but I need you to help set it up in my place. I would really like to decorate a tree this Christmas."

"If it's all right with you, I can pick up a ten-dollar permit from the Forest Service, and we can take a trip to the Arapaho National Forest," I said. The Arapaho National Forest was one of the first national forests established by Theodore Roosevelt in 1908, and it was just south of Elks Run. "They've designated areas that are open for cutting down trees. It really helps them thin out those areas, but we need to dress for the weather."

"Oh, that sounds great! I heard about that program. I guess it depends on your schedule," she said.

"The best time is during the week. It's much easier for me to get time off."

"Okay, I can do it on Thursday morning. How about you?" she said.

"Sure. Thursday morning is good for me unless there's a major issue with the computer system."

"On Wednesday night, I'll call you. Will Stanley be able to come?"

"I would like to take Stanley, but basset hounds had a tendency to pick up and follow a scent until there isn't any left. And it would be difficult for him to move in deep snow."

"I understand," she said.

"It'll be fun. I can't wait. Talk to you soon. Have a good night, Mike."

"Yeah, you too. See you soon."

*This will be fun.*

# Chapter 22

I checked the weather to make sure a blizzard wasn't in the works, but by the time we got to the forest, a severe cold front had dropped into the region. The day ended up being the coldest day on record. The temperature reached a bone-chilling ten below zero. The wind was unforgiving, but we had made a decision not to leave without a tree. We felled the nearest decent-looking six-foot tree. It was a quick stop, chop, and cop. We didn't see anyone else on the forest road.

*No wonder. What fool would drive out here on a day like today? Even the coffee in the thermos is cold.*

After I set up the tree in Diane's condominium and got the last string of lights on it, my phone beeped with a text message. The primary database was in trouble. It was running out of space. Damn it!

Diane made me a hot chocolate for my drive to the resort. She promised to decorate the tree and would call so that we could admire it with some wine and cheese.

I agreed wholeheartedly.

# Chapter 23

Christmas Eve was just two days away, and it was a tradition at Elks Run to see Old Saint Nick arrive in a horse-drawn sled. He visited all the kids and their parents in the main lodge.

The instructors and patrollers geared up for the torchlight parade down the main slope in front of the Heavenly Lodge. Ron and I had been in the last three parades. We used skis because of the wide turns and slow pace. The first year, we used red flares to light up the slope, but the flares caused burns on our hands and uniforms, and they left us gasping for air. We began using battery-operated torches.

Some of the instructors took it as a serious endeavor, but others laughed all the way down the slope. Maybe, it was the alcohol that was drunk beforehand, but we tried our best to focus on the skier in front of us and not take a shortcut through the woods. Our parade was executed perfectly without a hitch. No one took a fall or a shortcut through the woods.

When I was a kid, my parents took me to the Radio City Christmas Show in New York City to see the Rockettes. They had dressed up in military uniforms as they skated in formation around a center point. At the farthest point from the center, one Rockette was skating hard to keep up with the formation, and the audience was cheering for her to catch up.

I said, "I have to say that the parade looked great, especially those who will remain anonymous who waited until the end of the parade to celebrate."

Ron said. "I agree with you. Last year was an embarrassment, but maybe this was another good omen, along with the snow we're getting,"

"You may be right. Let's go over to the lodge to meet Ginny and Diane."

Inside, the lodge glittered with festive decorations. The smell of pine was in the air. Massive pinecone wreaths hung over the fireplaces and balconies. Large Colorado blue spruces were lit up with row after row of white lights. Wooden, silver, and gold ornaments hung from the branches. The resort guests and the employees mingled while the children met Saint Nick. His helpers—lift operators dressed as elves and reindeer—handed out candy canes and hot chocolate to all.

The happy spirit shown by everyone made everyone forget that Elks Run was a business. It was as if Disneyland had moved from California to the Rockies. Nevertheless, I really liked that time of the year.

Ron and I stopped by the bar and ordered two rum and cokes in celebration. We saw Diane and Ginny to the right of the stone fireplace. Since I had talked to the construction supervisor building the lodge, I knew that the stone came from a nearby quarry.

Ginny waved, and we headed in that direction. Ginny and Diane were festively dressed and looked great.

"Hey, the parade looked great!" Ginny said to us.

"From here, it looked so beautiful," Diane added.

I said, "It wasn't bad at all compared to the problems we had last year. Right, Ron?"

"It was probably because we told a few of the guys to cool the drinking or we would kick their asses," Ron said nonchalantly.

"Ron, you aren't serious, are you?" Diane asked.

Ron and I started laughing out loud, but he reassured Diane that we really told them to go easy on the drinks, but kicking their butts was in jest.

"Ginny, how do you know when these guys are telling the truth?" Diane said.

"Oh, I've gotten use to their jesting, and they wouldn't hurt a soul."

After Saint Nick finished greeting the children, the evening ended with everyone singing Christmas carols with a piano accompaniment. The joyful event ended with the singing of *Silent Night*.

I gave Ginny a hug and told her that I would stop by their house tomorrow evening with their gift.

Ginny turned to Diane and asked, "Diane, would you like to drop by our home tomorrow evening with Mike? Ron and I would like to have you over. I'm sure Mike would also."

"I exchange gifts with my parents, but if it's early, I would love to." She looked right at me as she answered.

"I cannot stay late because I need to be home for Stanley. Would five-thirty be all right?" I asked.

"That would be fine," Ginny said.

We gave each other another round of hugs, and Ginny gave me a wink.

As we walked toward the exit, Diane grabbed my hand and whispered, "They are truly nice friends."

I smiled and said, "They're the best."

# Chapter 24

"Hi, Mike. It's great to see you again," Diane said as I walked into her parents' home. She gave me a kiss, took my hand, and escorted me into the kitchen.

Her dad was talking to Brian Jones in the far corner, but he stopped the conversation and walked over to me. "Hi, Mike. I'm glad that you came to share our celebration. I should say that Diane was also excited that you came tonight."

"Oh, Dad. You are sometimes so dramatic," she said with a smile.

"Thanks for having me, Mr. Bunn. I brought a couple bottles of Barolo for you or your guests to enjoy."

"Thanks, Mike. I appreciate the gesture. Diane, please introduce Mike to your mother while I check on the food."

"Mom, I would like to introduce you to Mike Doyle."

"Mike, it's a pleasure to meet you. I've heard so many good things about you from Joe and the rest of his staff. The resort was so happy to have you manage those all-important databases."

"It's a pleasure to meet you, Mrs. Bunn. I appreciate you having me here tonight."

"Oh, call me Marilynn. And thank you for bringing the wine. It'll go well with the cheese and cracker appetizers we're serving tonight. Actually, it's a lifesaver because we just finished the last bottle of Bordeaux. Mike, you're my guest. Please enjoy our food and home. Diane, please take Mike on a tour of the house."

My first impression of Marilynn Bunn was one of genuine honesty. I felt that she was so proud of Diane, her accomplishments, and sharing her home with others.

It was great to see his staff in a relaxed atmosphere. Even in my first meeting with them, everyone seemed to get along well. While making my rounds with Diane, I noticed that Brian Jones was talking to Joe Bunn again. He was speaking in Joe's ear, frowning, and gesturing as though he trying to emphasize a point.

Joe patted him on the shoulder and poured him another scotch on the rocks. I turned to join Diane's conversation with Betty Owens.

The TV was on, and we watched the ball drop from Times Square. Even though we were two hours behind, we sounded out a wish of good cheer.

I felt a tap on my shoulder.

Diane grabbed my sweater, pulled me to her, and gave me a passionate kiss. "Happy New Year, Mike. Thanks for making this a great celebration for me."

"Thanks for making this an extra special night for me too." I held her tight and kissed her again.

It was very strange not to be holding Debbie, but I had to say I liked how my life was falling into place.

# Chapter 25

The abundance of snow surpassed any snowfall in the past three years. Road crews were busy keeping the roads open and sanded in and around Elks Run.

Ron and Ginny were so busy that they hired another helper to help Ron maintain, sharpen, and adjust the equipment. There had never been a season like this one for them.

The resort was doing so well, and parking was getting harder to find. Shuttle buses were being used to transport skiers from the town to the lodge.

Diane told me that the resort was thinking about running a chairlift shuttle from the town to the base lodge to help with parking and customer frustrations. We were spending a lot of time together, enjoying each other's company, and snowboarding in other areas. She liked to compare Elks Run to other resorts, but I just liked to ride.

We made dinner at her place, watched movies, and took Stanley for long walks. He liked the attention and enjoyed taking the elevator in her condominium. Anything was better than walking up stairs.

# Chapter 26

As I pushed the door open to the lockers, my cell phone beeped with a text message. The database or the e-mail server had received an error. I had forgotten to change the text message to say which one.

"Cathy, I need to run to the computer room. Can you spare me for a while?"

"Sure, Mike. When and if you get back, let me know. I may need your help today."

"No problem. I will." As I reached for the door handle, Ron was on the other side.

He said, "Mike, where's the fire—or are they giving out free beer somewhere?"

"No. I've got a problem with the system."

"Before you run away, I promised John Swan that I would attend the Forest Service meeting tonight at city hall, but I need to help Ginny organize our stock. She said that it's a mess, and only I can straighten it out."

"Ron, what am I going to do there? I don't own a physical business in town."

"You can go and represent me, our business. You have the same convictions and concerns that Ginny and I do about Elks Run and what they do. I trust you."

"Okay. I'll go. Can you feed Stanley tonight? I'll come by for him after the meeting."

"That's no problem. Just give us call if something comes up," he said.

In the computer room, I logged into the databases. Everything was all right, but one e-mail server had run out of room. *Crap, who is it now? Well, let me see. Yep, it's Brian Jones again. Okay, I can move this file off the server, compress it, and move it back to create more space on the server without adding another data file. That should do it. I need to change that text message alert so that I include e-mail server problems.*

I logged off and walked to Brian's office, hoping that he was in without scheduling an appointment through his secretary. I passed Joe Bunn's office and gave a wave to Janet Lee.

She smiled and waved back.

Brian's secretary was not at her desk, but I went ahead and peered into his office. He was at his desk, and I knocked on the door.

He looked up. "Hey, Mike. What's up?"

"I'm running into a small e-mail space problem, and I noticed that you're receiving and sending a large amount of e-mail attachments with graphics. I wondered if you could save those e-mail attachments to your hard drive or another storage device and not keep them in your personal e-mail folders. The problem I'm running into is that the e-mail server keeps on running out of space, and I keep extending the space. There's only a limited amount of space, and I know that we don't have the budget to buy more storage. I'm afraid that it may take down the entire e-mail system."

"Oh, sorry. Hell, I don't want to stop e-mails from coming in to the resort. You're right. I'll either save them to a hard drive or delete them. By the way, can you see the e-mails I am getting?"

No way was I going say that I did read some of his e-mails and knew where they were coming from. "No. I can't tell a thing. I just see that the space is being used."

"I understand. How are things going for you?"

"Great. I'm busy teaching and taking care of the system." I knew that he knew that I was dating Diane, but he didn't say anything about it. I was curious about the new gondola, and I asked whether the lift would be finished on time.

"Yes, we're on schedule, and we should be ready for that weekend. By the way, do you want to take a test ride and try skiing down from the top?"

"Can I bring a friend with me?"

"Not a problem. I think I'm going to do a test run next Thursday around noon. I'll send out an e-mail to the staff. Just check your e-mail at the beginning of the week."

I wanted to ask him about the late-night concrete work on the lift and whether there could be a problem with the towers, but I didn't. *Heck, what do I know?* "Great. Thanks for your time," I said as I left his office.

# Chapter 27

Walking down the stairs from Brian's office, I looked out the windows at a panoramic view of the slopes. I was hoping for a good powder day in the morning. It should happen. The counter-clockwise circular flow of air that generally comes up from the Gulf of Mexico and travels over Colorado during the winter hadn't disappointed us this year. The snow average for the state was huge! The snow base level for Elks Run was fifty-two inches. If it didn't snow for a day, the snow was blown. And when it snowed at night, the powder was fantastic in the morning.

To snowboard in powder feels surreal. When you learn to master powder, you're hooked and want nothing more than to ride it every day. It's like the cartoons where Aladdin glides effortlessly on his magic flying carpet. You're on a cushion of dry virgin snow that you glide over effortlessly. You don't feel the contact of your snowboard with the slope because it's floating on top of it in the snow. Your board could be in two feet of snow below the surface and it isn't touching the slope or the terrain. When skiing in powder, it's important that the slope is steep so that gravity can pull you through it. You don't want to fall or slow down. The snow may be soft, but digging out of it can be really hard. I know because I have fallen in some precarious places on my skis and my snowboard. It's one hell of a way to spend your day; people don't stop to help because doing so will cause them to get stuck in it too. You're on your own.

I called Diane and said, "How's your day going for you?"

"Just great, Mike. I've got a surprise for you tonight. I'm doing Italian, your favorite, and I stopped to pick up chews for Stanley. What time will you guys be over?"

"Sorry, Diane. Ron asked me to attend a town meeting to listen in on the Elks Run expansion. He and Ginny were behind on their work, and I guess I do owe them. I would need a calculator to add up the number of times they have taken care of Stanley."

"I understand, but it would have been nice if you had called me earlier. I started the sauce, but I can refrigerate it and save it for another day. Do you need me to take care of Stanley?"

"No thanks. Ron will feed him tonight. I'm really sorry that I did not call you sooner. If it's not too late, can I call you tonight?"

"Sure. Drive safe."

"Great. Love you."

"Love you too, Mike."

# Chapter 28

I arrived at city hall five minutes before the meeting started. At the entrance, I picked up the meeting agenda from the table. Looking around the hall, I saw many of the store owners already seated. John Swan had saved a seat for me.

"Mike, glad you can come. Where's Ron? I was expecting him."

"Sorry, Mike. I'm filling in for him. He and Ginny need to sort out some inventory issues. Do you know how long this meeting will last? I just gave up a perfectly good Italian dinner with Diane for this meeting."

"Sorry about that, but the meetings last about an hour or so, depending on the questions."

"Actually, I'm here for Ron to listen and learn as he would."

Mayor Spencer approached the podium. "May I have everyone's attention please? Many of you know me, but others may not. I'm Chris Spencer, the mayor of Elks Run. This was a scheduled meeting of a proposal from Elks Run Ski Resort to extend their land acreage from the present 225 acres to a proposed 275 acres. That would be an increase of appropriately fifty acres. The proposed area is located three-quarters of a mile from the Elks Run Resort entrance on the North Road and ends one-quarter mile short of South Willow Creek. The land will be developed as condominiums. All this information and much more is contained in the information packet. This is your time to voice your concerns or agreement to this proposal. I don't have to remind you of this because two times in the past you were part of Elks Run's expansion meetings. All of us read your remarks. When I say all of us, I mean the town council, the Forest Service, other citizens, and me.

"Tonight, Wally Bonnet, our regional forest service director and Roger Grim, Elks Run director of real estate and planning are present. Now, as always, we need to hear all sides of this issue in Elks Run, whether you favor one side or the other. If you like, you can mail, e-mail, or text me your comments, or leave them on our web site. Natalie Vogel, our illustrious editor said that the *Elks Run Daily* is covering these proceedings and offering, as always, her own insight. If you know Natalie, it's an unbiased as well as entertaining insight."

The room filled with clapping and laughter. Everyone in town knew that Natalie leaned toward preserving our forest landscape and made no bones about her position. She didn't want to see the town turn into a suburb of Denver. However, tourism and the homes that were bought in Elks Run were always welcome. She had irked the businesses of the town with many of her anti-business editorials.

Mayor Spencer said that most everyone present knew about the proposal and may have thoughts or questions on the issue for the Forest Service or Elks Run Resort.

Peter Rice, manager of Mountain Bank, approached the microphone and said, "I want to say that many business owners served by my bank have told me that they're looking forward to the expansion. It will help them economically, and the plan that the Forest Service and Elks Run put together seems to makes sense. It will preserve our landscape and our wildlife."

Many in the hall clapped in approval.

Joe Crop, PineTree's regional director, made his way to the podium. "Peter started by telling us all how wonderful the planning has been for this project. However, this meeting and others for the Elks Run expansions have been rubber-stamped under the guise of being real discussions about the issues. Roger, I sent you requests from recreation groups, other than skiers, who are concerned about their use of the land. That group includes hunters, anglers, hikers, and campers. They pay user fees for using the lands adjacent to Elks Run."

Roger said, "Joe, I looked into all group usage of the land, and the expansion will not jeopardize their use of public land."

"Did you have a chance to tell the anglers that even though the expansion will stop short of South Willow Creek from North Road, the creek will be dammed upstream from the expansion so that Elks Run would have more water flowing into its reservoir, and the water flow for the fish downstream will be negligible?"

Mayor Spencer, Wally Bonnet, and Roger Grim seemed as though they were all familiar with Joe Crop's questions.

Wally Bonnet said, "The Forest Service studied the water flow before and after the damming of South Willow Creek, and it varied by only two cubic feet per minute, which is satisfactory. In addition, the reservoir will be stocked with trout by the Forest Service."

"That's great, but will the reservoir be open to all anglers?"

"Since we do stock the reservoir for the benefit of anglers downstream, that decision will be made by Elks Run."

Roger Grim said, "That decision is forthcoming, but it most likely will be opened for downstream anglers."

*That's a copout, but that's what I expected from Roger. Whenever I need information from him, he is so aloof. His interest is in expanding present properties and buying others.*

Joe Crop thanked the mayor and returned to his seat. I thought his questions had been relevant and presented another point of concern.

A few other people asked questions on the impacts to the police, fire, water, and sewer services. When the questions ended for the general public, the Forest Service and Elks Run took about five minutes to summarize their planning. Elks Run explained the benefits it brings to the community.

Roger Grim said, "If the town council and the Forest Service approve the expansion, Elks Run Resort is going to subsidize up to 3 percent of the business tax for ten years for present and future business owners."

That brought many smiles. Ron and Ginny would certainly be happy, but would the town end up paying a price for this and any other future expansions?

# Chapter 29

John Swan asked if I would like to meet Joe Crop. I thought it might not be a good place to meet him, especially since Roger Grim had waved to me, but I said, "Okay John. But do me favor and don't tell him I work the computer systems at the resort."

"Sure. I hear you," he said as we walked toward John.

Natalie Vogel was asking him a few questions that he answered politely.

"John, I would like you meet my friend, Mike Doyle. He is a snowboard instructor at the resort."

"It's my pleasure to meet you, Mike. I am glad you came tonight. What did you think of the meeting?"

"To be honest with you, I'm here for Ron and Ginny Gustaff, owners of the best ski and bike shop in town," I said.

"I know that shop; it's great. I believe my wife and I took one of their bike trips to South Park a few years ago. What did you think about my questions tonight?"

"I have to say that you did give me another perspective on the issue."

"Mike, it's not just another perspective; it's for the balance of our resources and economy. I'm a conservationist who knows that we need to work with the Forest Service, the community, and the resorts to preserve our wilderness. To be honest with you, Elks Run doesn't want to cooperate on these issues. I believe they sway the Forest Service to do the same."

"John, weren't you responsible for blocking traffic and disrupting lift operations at this and other resorts throughout the this state and the country?" I asked without any thought whatsoever.

"We may have been guilty of disrupting operations at a few resorts, but we have never hurt a person or destroyed any property. That's not how we bring this matter to the attention of the community, state, or nation," he answered with a fire in his eyes that told me my questions with him had ended. "Mike, I need to get going. It was nice to talk with you. I wouldn't mind discussing these issues again. John knows where we meet weekly. It would be great to see both of you there," he said as he extended his hand to shake mine."

"Thanks for the invite," I said with a smile. *There is no way in hell I am going to attend any of his meetings.*

Joe headed to the exit accompanied by a few others who didn't look too friendly.

"John, I need to get a move on. Tomorrow looks like another big snow day. Plus, I need to take Stanley for a walk."

"I'm coming with you," he said as we headed out the door.

# Chapter 30

The weather was cold, and heavy snow was falling. However, there was a bright side to the weather. The skiing was terrific. During my time in Colorado, there hasn't been any bleak skiing years. Thank you, La Niña.

The opening of the gondola lift was a week away. The buzz was everywhere, including a huge banner strung across Main Street. From the Coffee Mug Café to the slopes, there was great anticipation. The best barometer was the amount of ski bookings. I had been checking the reservation numbers, and a couple of calculations showed me that the resort's numbers were about 30 percent higher than the previous two years. That was astonishing. The only thing I could bitch about was the traffic in town. It was everywhere. Whether I was home or with Diane, I needed extra time driving to get where I was going. I was so proud of Stanley. He adjusted to being shuttled between Ginny, Diane, and me. He loved to meet people and enjoyed all the attention.

While driving, I noticed that the heavy machinery, helicopters, men, and barricades were all gone from the staging area.

Ginny called and said, "Good morning, Mike. I probably didn't hear you, but do you have Stanley with you or did you forget to drop him off," she asked.

"I thought I told you that he's with me today. I need to work on some computer stuff, and I thought I would give you a break today. Diane said she could take care of him tomorrow. She needs to take a break from the lift opening. I can't tell you how many times she has recited exactly how the opening is going to take place in case I see any problems. At this point, I really don't need to be at the opening. Thanks for your call. I'll see you soon."

The snow had picked up, and there were at least six inches on the ground. The snowplows were crossing in all directions.

Stanley and I made our way to the instructor lockers. He reminded me of a Coast Guard boat plowing its way through fifteen-foot waves for a rescue. Finally, reaching the building overhang, I was able to brush the snow off him and me. He loved the snow; if his legs were about two feet longer, he would have made a great avalanche dog. I don't know whether everyone was ecstatic to see him or just happy for the snow and the extra business it generated. Maybe, it was a little of both.

In the farthest corner of the room, a high-pitched voice said, "Stanley."

Stanley looked over, and Ron was on his knees, waiting to greet him.

Stanley rolled over on his back, and Ron rubbed his belly. Stanley found the hidden treat in his shirt pocket, and Ron stood up.

"I assume that you're staying in today," he said.

"Yes. I need to check up on things. By the way, Joe Bunn gave me a little more responsibility. He wants me to take over the resort's website. The company that created the site went out of business, and it needs to be updated. I signed another contract to manage it."

"That's great, but I can tell by your expression that you don't seem too happy about it."

"I have mixed feelings because I don't get to snowboard as much as I did in the past. I can't teach as many lessons. Cathy isn't counting on me as much now, but I'm able to spend more time with Stanley and Diane."

"There you go. That's the way to think about it. You know lessons are sometimes a pain in the butt. I'm happy that we have the shop. I love the shop and spending time with Ginny. I love to ski too, and so do you. When you have the chance to ski and enjoy the mountain, it's a special moment. Enjoy it as if it's the last time. Speaking of lessons, I've got to get to one in a few minutes."

"Sure. Ginny said to tell you not to forget your lunch today."

"She is something special. Okay. I need to go. Stanley, you better watch out for your dad." Ron got down on his knees to get a few more licks.

"Be careful, Ron," I said as he headed for the door.

There were only a few stragglers rushing out the door for the slopes.

# Chapter 31

Stanley and I made our way down the two flights of stairs to the computer room. The room was a little chilly for the benefit of the servers. I turned on a small electric heater near my desk and pressed the play button on the cassette player, which I put in Stanley's new therapeutic mattress bed. The pad fit nicely under my desk. It had channels with ridges in it that were specially made for a dog's body. Stanley had the same one at home, but this one had a great red plaid cover. Once, I was so tired that I used it as a pillow while Stanley slept on it.

I could tell that the holiday was coming because of all the e-mail traffic on the mail servers. I didn't have a budget for additional storage, but Joe Bunn had found some money that allowed me to purchase and install another ten-terabyte-storage drive.

Since putting the storage drive online, I hadn't seen many space issues. The space needs of the e-mail servers had doubled since I came aboard, but that was probably the result of all the correspondence between the resort and the rest of the world. Diane had told me it took hours to answer her e-mails. I was happy that I wasn't that important.

Joe Bunn had asked the staff to attend the ribbon-cutting ceremony Monday. I had promised Diane that if we could take the gondola to the top, we would snowboard down on the blue runs. She said that she would try to arrange it. Since her first lesson, she had worked on improving her skills; it was fun being on the slopes with her. It reminded me of the fun I had with Debbie when we skied.

*Oh, I forgot that Debbie and Jessica are thinking about making it here to ski. Let me write a note to Cathy and have her drop a few passes into Ron's locker. I hope Debbie can make it this time because I am reaching my limit on free passes for the season.*

*Let me see. E-mail servers and their backups are running fine. The primary and secondary databases are in sync, and there are no problems with the backups. What happened to the music?*

Stanley had stepped on the stop button with his big paw. "Nice job, Stanley."

He looked at me with a look that said he didn't mean it.

"Okay, Stanley, I am almost finished here. Give me a minute."

He walked to the door and sat down.

I ran a couple of SQL scripts, and the results look fine. I didn't want to have any issues with the opening. "Okay, Stanley. How about you and me head home."

# Chapter 32

When the alarm rang at 6:30, Stanley was more startled than I was. It was earliest that either of us had gotten up in a very long time.

"This is payback for all the times I've heard you whine while I was sleeping."

He looked at me with big, droopy, bloodshot eyes.

I needed to get ready quickly. The gondola official opening ceremony was at ten, and Diane didn't want to be late. It was amazing how fast Stanley and I could move when we needed to; in minutes, we were on our way to pick her up.

There were more cars on the main road; the town seemed really alive for seven in the morning.

Ron and Ginny were going to open the shop at 7:30. Customers were lined up for their equipment as Stanley and I strolled in through the front door. Naturally, Stanley had to scent and greet everyone in the shop before I was able to reach Ginny and Ron.

Ron said, "Today is the big day. Are you ready for the ceremony, Mr. VIP?"

"Oh, come on. If it wasn't for Diane, I don't think you would see me dragging my butt out of bed this early."

"You may have a point there."

"But love does make getting up a little easier," Ginny chimed in.

"Is that something you guys have in common?" I asked with a sly smile.

"Yes—something like that." Ginny looked at Ron. "We'll save that for another episode of *Dr. Phil*."

Ron was playing with Stanley on the floor.

"Say hello to Diane for us," Ginny said as she gave me another hug.

Ron stood up. "I may not be able to take Blue Sky today with all my level-four lessons. Come on by and tell me about it."

"I will." I leaned down to give Stanley a big pat on his head. "I'll see you soon, my big handsome guy."

Diane was waiting for me in the middle of the street in front of her condo. "About time. I was getting ready to drive myself." She got in with her gear and gave me a hug and a kiss.

"Stanley and I moved as fast as we could, and that was hard to do."

"My boys had to get up so early? I am so proud of you," she said with a giggle.

"By the way, Ron and Ginny say hi."

"They must be very busy this morning."

"They are. And Stanley greeted every customer."

"I am so excited for the skiers, the town, Elks Run, and for my dad. I hope everything goes well today."

"Me too, but I think we're hitting our first roadblock." There was a maze of car lights and flashing police lights. "It looks like PineTree is also excited about the opening."

Diane looked as if she seen a ghost and reached for her cell phone. "I need to call my dad to see if he made it in. My mom said that he was leaving earlier than usual this morning."

Before she could dial, her phone rang.

"Dad, how are you? We are about a quarter mile from the resort. Yes, we're all right. Oh, that's good. Is everything on schedule? Great! We will see you soon. Love you too. Bye. Dad said that Chief Trent made a few arrests, and the road should open soon. You were right; it is PineTree. If the police need any other help, Dad said he was willing to pay for the sheriff or the state police."

"Everything will be fine, especially when we board down from the top." I gave her a big hug.

"Thanks, Mike."

The traffic started moving slowly, and I saw Bob Trent handcuffing Joe Crop. He and a few other protesters had chained themselves to the guardrails on either side of the road and daisy-chained themselves across the road. A number of protesters were carrying signs saying that Elks Run

Resort and the Forest Service had trampled on the rights of nature, and the expansion of the resort must stop. Two Summit County sheriffs were sorting out the mess.

"Get a life. These people don't realize the quality of life the resort brings to all who live here and the amount of time we spend on environmental studies. Dad was right that you can't reason with them. What do you think?"

"I was thinking about taking a scenic ride on Blue Sky and riding the bowl."

"You are so nonpolitical; maybe that's why I love you." She laughed and said, "It's still going to be a great day."

I had never seen the parking areas so full at 8:15.

Diane reached for her snowboard boots and laced them up. "I hate to leave you, but drop me off at the local TV truck. I need to coordinate my dad's interview with them and the Denver affiliate. You are going to be on time for the ribbon-cutting ceremony, aren't you?"

"Yes. I need to check some things out, but I am not going to miss it."

"You better not!" she said, and then she kissed me.

"Break a leg for me—and I don't mean that literally."

"Thanks. See you soon."

# Chapter 33

I found a parking spot and ran into the administration building.

Joe Bunn said, "I see that you and Diane were able to get past the road blockage in one piece. Will you be able to make it to the ribbon-cutting ceremony?"

"Yes, Mr. Bunn, but I need to check a few things out first. By the way, Diane was talking to the TV stations and arranging your interviews with them."

"Okay, thanks." Joe turned to Brian Jones and said in a low tone of voice, "Brian, make sure the towers are covered for this week."

"Joe, I took care of everything." It didn't take me long to check out the servers and databases and head toward the Blue Sky lift with both snowboards. Lots of people were lined up, but I flashed my ID and went right past them. Being part of the staff did have its rewards. A live band near the main lodge was pumping up the crowd.

As I maneuvered around the TV crews, I saw Diane talking to her Dad. He had finished an interview with one station and was on his way to the other one from Denver. I said, "Diane, how's it going?"

"It's been crazy. I can't believe the amount of people waiting to take this lift. Thanks for bringing my board. Dad is doing well. Mom called not too long ago and said that she is driving up to have lunch with me. Do you mind?"

I was amazed how someone could say so much without taking a breath. It had to be adrenaline. I said, "That's fine."

She gave me a hug. "It's almost ten. We should make our way to the ribbon."

The ribbon extended from the lift loading point with the shiny gondola not far in the background.

Joe Bunn took over and moved everyone around so that we were all in the picture for the resort photographer. The eight-inch-wide ribbon was lowered just a little, and the camera snapped twice.

Diane called someone on her two-way radio and said the band should begin the countdown.

The band asked the waiting crowd to start the countdown. The pumped-up crowd needed no help and began the countdown in earnest.

When they reached one, Joe Bunn cut the ribbon. Cheers rang out, and the band started playing again. Joe shook hands with his staff, hugged Diane, and walked over to the loading area. He greeted the first twelve skiers who would ride the lift. They carried their skis and boards to the gondola.

I turned to Diane and said, "I hope we don't have to wait too long— or else the powder will only be in our dreams.

She agreed and made a call on her two-way radio. "I took care of everything. Let's go."

I handed Diane her board, and she guided us to the lift. She waved to the lift operator and motioned to him that she would like to jump the line. He gave us a sign and held back two people.

The gondola doors slid open, and we boarded in thirty seconds. The doors closed quietly, and we began our ascent. The car was quite roomy for twelve people, and rock music played in the background. The ride was smooth, especially when it passed under a tower.

We had a great view of the resort, the town, and Eisenhower Tunnel.

As I looked down at the terrain, I noticed activity around the tower bases. It looked as though crews were covering the bases. Each base had a barrier fence to protect the skiers. The canvas cover was over the cement base. Just above the front window was a digital elevation and temperature readout.

At 10,110 feet, the temperature was twelve degrees, but the car was heated.

"Mike, this is just fantastic. I never dreamed that this view would be so spectacular. I asked the photographers to start taking pictures this winter and summer from the lift for a new brochure. What do you think?"

"You couldn't ask for a better view in the entire county. It looks like we will be arriving at the summit. Just ahead is the debarking area. Are you ready to have some fun?"

"You bet!"

The music interrupts by an announcer saying, "We hope you enjoyed the ride. Have a safe day skiing the back bowls of Elks Run."

The ride from the base at 9,400 feet to 12,277 at summit took eight minutes. Not bad at all.

As the door slid open, we grabbed our snowboards. The temperature was ten degrees.

# Chapter 34

From the summit, I saw the Gore Range, the White River, the Tenmile Range, and Loveland Pass.

"Mike? Mike, earth to Mike."

"Oh, sorry, just daydreaming."

"I bet. It's probably that blonde snowboarder you were looking at."

"Yeah, she was hot." I turned around, and a snowball hit me square in the chest. "Okay, okay. I was just admiring the view. Double diamond?"

"Funny. I want to live for another ride up."

"Okay, let's take Fantasy down to the quad lift. Remember to keep yourself balanced on the board."

"Enough already. Let's just go!" Diane started down the moderately steep blue trail; within twenty-five yards, she did a face plant and was buried in powder.

I got to where she was, pulled her up by her shoulders, and rolled her upslope. "Are you okay?"

"I am sorry. I guess I got too cocky." She was coughing up snow and trying to catch her breath.

"What I was going to say before you left was to stay balanced on the board, exaggerate your up motion for direction, and put a little more weight on the back of the board. I guess you know that now." I helped her brush off the snow, put her square on the board, and straightened her helmet. "Okay, the trail was wide. Let's try to board parallel to each other."

The rest of the run went great. After the powder run to the bottom of the front bowl, we were on a high and wanted more. We took another run down the same trail because the other skiers, except for a few areas within the trees, had swept the powder away.

After the runs, we took the quad lift up to Clouds Lodge at the top of the front bowl, cuddled up to the giant rock fireplace, and enjoyed hot chocolate. She said, "I am starting to feel every bone in my body. I guess I was not in the best shape like I thought I was. Now I know how you feel when you teach classes all day. How are you doing?"

"Not so bad. But if I don't start the trip down soon, I may not want leave."

"Well, we don't have to. Since I am the assistant to the director of marketing, I believe it would be in the resort's best interests to determine whether the Blue Sky lift is a summer tourist attraction. What better way than to take the car down from the summit. It would be a romantic ride down. Don't you agree?"

"Diane, you're a genius. I thought about faking an injury, but they would send a snowmobile up, and that's no fun. Let's do it."

We went to the loading station and asked for a ride. After a little persuasion by Diane, we were off. The ride down was just as breathtaking, but it was little more romantic than the ride up. At the bottom, the attendants knew we were coming and stopped the car before it loaded skiers for the ride up.

We surprised the waiting skiers; one yelled, "Are you afraid of heights?"

With a smile and a wave, we headed to the lodge.

From a distance, I heard my name called. It was Debbie. "Hi, Mike. Are you busy? I left a message on your cell phone that Jessica and I would be coming up today for the opening. Are the comp passes still available?"

Diane said, "Oh, Deb. I am sorry, but in the rush to make the ribbon-cutting event this morning, I left them at home. I can get another pair for you and Jessica."

I said, "I'd like to introduce you to Diane Bunn. Diane, this is Debbie Shaw. Diane is the assistant to the resort's director of marketing."

"Diane, it's my pleasure to meet you. Mike, I need to touch base with Jean. Can we talk later? Debbie, it was very nice to meet you."

Diane and Debbie smiled at each other.

"Mike, I apologize for startling you and Diane. She is very cute."

"No, it's my fault for not carrying a phone. And we're just friends. We met in a snowboard lesson. Let's walk to the ticket office to get another set of comp tickets. How are you doing?"

"Same work, but more of it. Jessica and I help each other out. The guys all have big egos and don't want to be seen helping a female colleague. My clients think I am doing a great job for them, and that's what counts for me. You still look like you're in excellent shape. How is the job with the resort going?"

"The job is going well. The opportunity just dropped in my lap, and I am grateful for it. I sometimes spend more time in a computer room than on the slopes, but it gets old picking up students."

"You never liked that, but it seems as though your business is growing. I am happy for you and Stanley. How is Stanley?"

"He's fine. He has been a fixture at the shop. Ginny had skiers asking whether he was in today. I am so grateful that Ron and Ginny can help."

"I know. They are the best. I would like to drop by and see Ginny, Ron, and Stanley on my way home. Even though I work out at the company gym as often as I can, I don't think my muscles are ready for a long day of skiing."

"Sure. Drop by the shop. I am sure they'd all love to see you. I don't think Ron will be there. Ron works almost every day. Don't spend too much time on your skis, especially if this is your first day. I don't want to see you as a casualty." I really didn't want to see any harm come to her. Even though we had our issues, I still liked her in her own way. "By the way, did you do something to your hair?"

"I thought a shorter cut might be easier to take care of in the morning. I haven't really gotten used to it."

"I think it looks great."

"Thanks Mike."

At the ticket office, I showed my ID and got the comp passes. "Here are the passes. I hope you and Jessica have a great day of skiing."

"Thanks again."

I got this feeling, and I went for it. "I don't know whether you would like come up another day and have dinner with me at TT's. If you feel uncomfortable, Jessica can join us."

The silence only lasted a few seconds, but it felt like a minute.

"It would have to be a weekend, but I would like to."

"Cool. Leave me a message or send an e-mail when you can come up."

"Sure. I'll try to give you a week in advance, barring any emergency court appearances. I better find Jessica at the ski rack before she starts worrying. Have a safe day."

"You too, Debbie," I said. The days of popcorn and ice cream in bed flooded my mind.

# Chapter 35

I needed to think about what had happened earlier with Debbie. We had spoken on the phone, but I hadn't seen her in nearly four months. She seemed different, and her haircut looked great and so did she. She seemed to be able to differentiate between business and pleasure. That had been an issue before our divorce.

I decided to stop at a bar on the way to Ron and Ginny's. Bob's Place had a couple of pool tables, smelled of secondhand smoke, made good burgers, and the one TV only played sports. I hadn't seen the owner for some time, and it would be nice to say hello.

Pulling in front of the bar, there were only a few cars. Walking in, I got a few stares from the guys at a pool table.

I gave them a smile and took one of the open seats at the bar. "Mike Doyle, how the hell are you?" Bob said with a big smile. Bob was about my size, but his shoulders and biceps are twice as large as mine. "How's your wife and that dog? Stanley, right?"

Reaching over the bar to shake his hand, I said, "Stanley is doing fine, but Debbie and I got a divorce in the fall."

"Sorry to hear that. What can I get you?"

"How about a Coors Light. How has business been for you?"

"I hate to say it, but Elks Run has taken some of my business. I still have some local folk, but others died or moved to Arizona. Heck, I am getting old and tired of the snow. I might move there and join them." He acknowledged another customer and walked to the far end of the bar.

As I was watching the Colorado Avalanche game on TV, I felt a hand on my right shoulder. "Hi, Mike. Do you remember me?"

"I believe your name is Joe Crop. We met at the town hall meeting."

"That's right. What brings you to Bob's Place?" He took a seat next to me.

"I need to think a little bit and maybe catch a little of the Avalanche game." I hoped he would get the hint, but I fired from both barrels and said, "Joe, this morning, as I was traveling up Resort Road, I saw you being put into a patrol car. I assume that it was for disrupting traffic on the Blue Sky lift opening. Am I correct?"

"You are right. I received a misdemeanor summons. This is how we bring this matter to the attention of the community, state, and nation. I concede that the lift is there to stay and will only come down in a natural disaster. I am concerned about expansion to the north and east. The resort's townhouses and condominiums kill the wildlife ecosystems like a parasite. This parasite feeds on growth and greed for the sake of recreation. Please don't tell me that the town meetings are democratic and all sides represent each other equally. Can you honestly say that the last one was? If so, you are probably drinking a lot more than Coors Light."

"I can't answer your question because that was the first one I ever attended. Therefore, I have no previous experiences to base it on. Now that I am a resident of the county, I will probably attend a lot more. I know you understand that there are many people, including your friends, who are employed by the resort and other businesses. Most of those people are local or possibly travel over Loveland or Hoosier Passes to get here. I don't think they can afford the drive to Denver. Believe it or not, we need the people from Denver—or any other place on the planet—to purchase condominiums and townhouses so the tax base stays low. Heck, I have friends who live in a modest home in Aspen that they purchased in the seventies. They pay a couple hundred dollars for real estate tax. Why? Because the rich and famous pay the highest taxes on their million-dollar vacation homes and subsidize the real estate taxes. To me, that's fair."

"So I should roll over and not protect the rights of deer, trout, elk, and the aspen trees? They don't have a voice, do they?"

I looked at my watch and knew this conversation wasn't going anywhere fast. "Joe, I need to leave, and it isn't because of you. I have to get an early start tomorrow morning, and I hope that I don't see you lying down on the road again."

"I can't guarantee it, but the impression I want you to leave with is that I am truly dedicated to the preserving as much of the wildlife and its ecosystems—and I want all of us to enjoy it. In addition, I want to squash all rumors that say PineTree uses intimidation or dangerous tactics to get our points across. Emphatically, my group doesn't."

"I hope what you're saying is true because I want to believe you. I really need to get up early; maybe we can talk again another time."

"Sure, Mike. See you soon." He walked back to a group playing pool. "Goodnight, Bob. I'll try to make it back soon."

"Mike, it was good to see you. Drive safe."

Since I hadn't been able to do much serious thinking about Debbie there, I'd try again before I picked up Stanley.

# Chapter 36

The phone alarm rang with a background cry of a whimpering basset hound.

"Stanley, see who's at the door?" I said as if this would make him stop whimpering. Sometimes it worked, but not that time. "Okay, okay. I'm getting up." I tried twice to stand up, making it up on the third try. *Oh, I can see this is going to be great day.*

"Hi, Ginny, Mary has Ron left already?"

"Yep. He was excited about a lesson that was taking him to the top of Blue Sky," Ginny said with a smile. "I was getting tired of hearing him say that his lessons weren't bringing him to the top."

"Oh, he'll totally enjoy it. Heck, he may never come down."

"I don't think so, Mike. He has a tendency to show up whenever I cook. Cooking a meal means Ron is showing up. It works every time." Ginny rang up another sale.

I said, "I am working today, but I'll see what comes my way. I did take Stanley for a long walk. I think we will take a drive to the warehouse to pick up a few extra skis and snowboards for rental."

Ginny looked down at Stanley. When Stanley hears the words "treat" or "ride," he wouldn't let me out of his sight.

"Mike, do you have a minute." Ginny grabbed my arm and took me to the back room. "I need to tell you that Debbie stopped by yesterday. She said that you two had a chat. She said that she accepted your invitation for dinner. You know I like Debbie, and I don't want to taint your opinion of this dinner, but I could tell she was happy that she accepted it. It reminded me of the smiles she had when I first met the two of you. I feel much better after telling you. I was sure that you also wanted to have this dinner with her. Ron and I wish both of you the happiest no matter the outcome of this dinner or in the future."

"I can only hope that when we sit down and talk about how this all happened, we can understand whether it was the right move. Maybe, after getting this understanding, we can try to repair it or look toward the future. Thank you for telling me." I gave her a hug.

"I don't want to take all the credit, but I think there was something in Debbie's words that led me to believe she wouldn't mind me telling you." She gave me a wink.

"Oh, that's great. Really great." I smiled back. "Okay, Stanley, take care of Ginny today. I'll see you this afternoon, okay?"

Stanley looked up at me, and I gave him a big hug.

"Can you take on an intermediate snowboard class of about six students since I haven't seen you in action for most of the season?" Only Cathy could say something so sarcastically without even cracking a smile.

"I guess you will have to trust me. Am I going to the top?"

"See how it goes, but you're welcome to the take the blue trails down. I certainly can use you the next couple of days—if you can break away from the computer room."

"I need to get away and teach a little more. I'll try to help out."

"Thanks. Any help is welcomed. Go get them."

The class was going quite well, and everyone was concentrating on their linked turns. I told them that their reward for doing well was a ride on the Blue Sky lift.

We finished our run down to the main lodge, and I got a big "all right" from everyone when we headed toward the gondola. I took myself out of my bindings and reminded everyone to make sure that they carried water to hydrate themselves.

I signaled to the car loader that I needed to be in the same car with my students, and he gave me the thumbs-up. A siren went off, and red lights swirled inside and outside the lift control center. I looked at my watch; it was eleven. The first thought that came to my mind was that it was a problem with offloading at the top, but that wouldn't sound a siren.

Cathy radioed the instructors who were near the base lodge to excuse themselves from their students and immediately go to the ski patrol office. We were to tell our students that they would need to report to the ski school desk to get a make-up voucher for the lesson or a full refund.

Strapping my board over my shoulder, I told my students that I needed to go to the ski patrol office; when everything was all sorted out, I would continue the lesson. They seemed concerned, but they hoped that everything would be all right.

John Prescott, ski patrol director, and Bob Ryan were there with a number of ski patrollers and instructors. Six snowmobiles and four snow cats were pointing uphill with engines running. John invited all of us to take a seat in the office. He positioned himself in front of a map of the trail system, turned on a laser pointer, and said, "Gentlemen and ladies, we had one or possibly two towers collapse on the Blue Sky. The towers may or not be on the ground, which means there may be two cars in the air or on the ground. I'll get verification when the Flight for Life helicopter from St. Ambrose Memorial does a quick reconnaissance of the area. The helicopter will be at our disposal until the operation is complete.

"Depending upon the injuries to the skiers, I will coordinate the Summit County Ambulance, the Red, White, and Blue Fire Department, the Summit County Sheriff's Office, and the county's search and rescue team. Doctor John Hanes and his staff from St. Ambrose will handle the triage for the skiers involved in the collapse. We need to make sure that we can account for all skiers in every car that's on the ground or stuck in the air. We'll compare those numbers to the lift operator's load count.

"We need to get statements from everyone—no matter how unimportant it may seem to them. The operations center said that there was no signal from tower fourteen and fifteen. Therefore, I am going to assume that it's those two towers. After we safely evacuate the skiers from those cars, the snow cats will go to the top of Blue Sky to transport down the remaining skiers from both bowls, including the Clouds Lodge staff. We don't want to have anyone ski down from the lodge because there will be no patrollers on the slope.

"We want to account for everyone, and we need to secure the area for our preliminary investigation, Sky Stream, our insurance company, and others. I don't know how long this may take, and your help in staying on for a longer shift may be necessary, but I understand if you cannot stay longer. The rest of the mountain will operate as usual until we can safely close each section down. I want to see a show of hands of all patrollers and instructors who took the car rescue training this past summer."

I raised my hand along with a few instructors and most of the patrollers. The car rescue training was intense and involved knowing knots and belaying techniques. We couldn't be afraid of heights.

Three rescuers climbed up the lift tower steps that were nearest to the stuck car with safety ropes. One rescuer would clip in with safety ropes in the middle of the way up the tower. The second rescuer would clip in on top of the tower. A trolley bar mechanism would clip onto the lift wire that carried the car.

Under the bar, the third rescuer would sit in a sturdy chair with safety lines and turn a small wheel with his arms in a circular motion. A special braking system would keep the trolley from spinning out of control in either direction. When he positioned himself over the car, he could lower himself on top of it.

A special door on top of the car would open from the top. He carried a rope ladder that he lowered into the car. One at a time, each person in the car would climb up the ladder, be clipped into the chair, and be controlled by the rescuer on top of the car until he or she reached the tower. The rescuer on the tower would provide safety clips so the skiers could climb down the tower steps to the next rescuer. That rescuer would give encouragement and check rope security while helping the person reach the bottom of the tower.

The ski patrol would take them to the bottom of the mountain. The toughest part was encouraging the skiers in the car to climb up the ladder and get them over to the tower. The second toughest part was asking them to leave their skis or snowboards with us until we could get their equipment off the car.

# Chapter 37

When I turned around to join the others for a ride to the towers, I saw Ron. "Ron, it's good to see you."

"Yeah, it's good to see you too. Ginny called me because she heard the siren in town and saw the emergency vehicles driving up to the resort. She was worried. She asked me about you, but I didn't know. I'll call her as we walk to say that you're all right."

Eight of us rode up together, but other than the sound of the engine, it was silent. We all looked at each other with disbelief. Driving up an established work crew road west of the tower, it didn't look as though there were any problems. When we took a ninety-degree turn and pushed through some heavy snow, we saw that tower fourteen was leaning off the base at a forty-five-degree angle. It was held up by twisted wires from tower fifteen, which was at a thirty-degree angle and touching the pine trees on the side of the tower trail.

Car number twenty-six was hanging about a hundred feet off the ground. It was not level, and the tower wires were pulling it to the left. The skiers and their equipment were jammed inside to the left. They were trying to move to the other side of the car. The car was rocking, which could cause tower fourteen to break the one remaining steel bar holding it to the base.

Brian Jones was looking at the base and putting caution tape around it. He was looking at the two remaining steel bars and the nuts near the base of the tower.

A ski patroller picked up a bullhorn and said, "This is the ski patrol. I plan to get you out of the car, but I need your cooperation." He pointed the bullhorn in the direction of the car.

There were faint voices coming from the car.

"All rescuers, please stop making noises. I need to hear the skiers in the car."

"Yes. We can hear you," said a voice from the car. "Do you have kids in the car? How many are with you?"

"No, there aren't any kids, and there are six of us in here."

I was not an expert, but by looking at the twisted tower wires, I could tell the typical car rescue system wasn't going to work. The tower wires were twisted. I guess we needed to go to another plan.

"Okay, a rescuer is going to come down on top of the car and open a door on top of it. One at a time, climb to the top of the car using the ladder he will drop down to you. He is going to put safety ropes on you. Please, one step at a time, climb down to us on the longer rope ladder. For your safety, do not look down. Look up at the rescuer on top of the car."

As the slow process of rescuing the skiers from car twenty-six began, Bob Ryan said, "Ron, Mike, you're both trained in the car rescue system, right?"

We nodded.

"The ski patrol is working with search and rescue on this car and the other car at tower fourteen. We could certainly use your skills for the other cars up to the top from this point. We have the lower elevation covered. I'll try to be in contact with all instructors. Are you willing to work six hours on and six hours off throughout the night or until we can evacuate all the skiers from the cars?"

We both said it wouldn't be a problem.

I was happy that Stanley was with Ginny. Diane was probably trying to communicate with the media and doing other things around the resort. Stanley would be the last thing on her mind.

Ron and I needed to do our jobs as professionally as possible and hope no one had been severely hurt. We climbed into a snow cat that was going up to tower fifteen. Passing the base of tower fourteen, I saw something very strange. The screws and bolts that held down the steel bars were gone. They had been there a couple of minutes earlier, and Brian was gone.

The car was wedged between the trees. Search and rescue teams were using chainsaws to cut down a few trees. At tower fifteen, the caution tape was already around the base tower. The base had been split in two pieces with the steel bars and no holding nuts. It seemed strange to me, and I mentioned it to Ron. He didn't remember seeing the nuts on the steel bars or on the base. A quick calculation said that there were nine towers and eighteen cars left to the top. That maybe about another 144 skiers. It was going to be a long cold night.

In six hours, we rescued five cars. We had no serious injuries, but a few people suffered some mild hyperthermia. Before leaving the ski patrol hut, we handed out a box of hand warmers to the rescued skiers.

The word from towers fourteen and fifteen were that the most serious injuries were concussions and a few broken bones. I was somewhat relieved, but my thoughts went out to any skiers with concussions. The accident could have been more tragic.

Ron and I were drained from working on the rescues, but we were rewarded with many thanks from all the skiers. I was able to get a few minutes of sleep, and I just wanted to sleep in the heated machine.

"Mike, wake up." Ron shook my shoulder.

We walked into the ski patrol hut, which was serving as the Incident Command Center or ICS. After being debriefed, we were released.

"Let's get some food," Ron said.

We passed a group of volunteers working under lights and wished them the best as they tried to rescue the remaining skiers.

Near the main lodge, workers guarded a skier equipment area. A Flight for Life helicopter waited in the parking lot in front of the main lodge, and specialists were on standby in Denver and Colorado Springs. In the lodge, I saw a section for emergency/rescue dining. To the right, there was another area for rescued skiers. There was a curtained area to the left for triaging the injured.

Ron and I sat down at a table near a fireplace for a little warmth. Before we took off our wet jackets, our hostess approached us and said, "Hi, guys. My name is Laura. I would like to thank you for helping with the accident. There's no cost for your meal, and you can order breakfast, lunch, or dinner. Do you know what you'd like to order? If not, I can bring you a menu."

"I think both of us would like to have the breakfast special," Ron said.

"I'll bring a pot of coffee out in a couple minutes."

I said, "It seems as though every contingency was covered. I didn't think we were so well prepared."

"Other than a few egos, I agree with you."

Ron called Ginny and said, "Yes, Mike is with me. We're having breakfast now. I'll be at the shop in an hour. Okay, love you."

Laura brought our breakfasts and the pot of coffee.

Ron said, "Ginny tells me that the police think that the towers were sabotaged. I asked her, and she said it came from a reliable police source."

"How in the world could they come to that conclusion? We just came down from the mountain, and there are a number of skiers still waiting to be rescued. Who did the preliminary investigation?" I asked.

"I don't know, but let's wait until tomorrow."

"Okay. I need to visit the computer room, and I will pick up Stanley in the next hour."

"I need to find out more about the equipment in the secured area because Ginny said that we're missing a few skis and snowboards. Mike, we have an extra cot at the shop. Why don't you come over and we can leave together in six hours if they need us."

"That sounds great," I said.

"Just come through the back door. Here's the key. I think you and I need sleep. I wouldn't stay here too long."

"I'll try not to."

We finished our coffee and headed in different directions.

# Chapter 38

E ven though all the lights were on in administrative building, I didn't pass anyone. While waiting to log into the databases, I checked my phone messages.

Debbie's was first. "Mike, the news reported a collapsed lift tower on the gondola lift at the resort. Are you and Ron all right? I cannot believe that such an accident could happen. I'll follow the news, but maybe you can give me a call. Talk to you soon."

Diane's was next. "Mike, are you all right? I cannot tell you how awful I feel about this accident. Dad was walking around in a daze. He said that this couldn't be an accident. I believe him. I know that you are helping the rescue effort. Please call me whenever you can. Love you."

The last message was my mom. "Mike, are you all right? I heard on the afternoon news about an accident at a Colorado ski resort. Is that where you work? The weather here is cold and damp. Aunt Betty is not feeling too well. It's her arthritis. I am okay, but I have some aches and pains. I hadn't heard from you. I hope you're all right. Give me a call when you can. Love, Mom." My mom can tell me a lot in a few short sentences.

I didn't see anything unusual on the database management console screen except for a lot of data log activity between the primary and secondary databases. Because of the tower problems, the mountain monitoring software was in overdrive, writing alerts in the database and sending e-mails and text messages. By logging into the application, anyone could see the graphic information on the screen.

*Let me look. The increased log activity started at 10:25. But what time was the first alert? I know the lift warning light and siren went off at 11:00.*

*That's when I looked at my watch. Wait a minute, why am I doing all this? What am I trying to prove? It was an accident, but Ginny alluded to something other than an accident. Okay, maybe someone received alerts about the towers and waited too long to stop the lift. I went over to another desk and picked up the binder that had information about the software. Using that information, I ran queries against the database to find the exact time of the first alert. It was 10:15. A forty-five-minute gap before the lift toppled. Why did operations wait so long? I was tired, but I needed to run one more query. When a tower has a problem, where is the alert sent? What? Brian Jones and Joe Bunn received e-mails and text messages? I might be reading too much into this, but Brian did have the tower areas roped off before the rescuers arrived.*

I started to nod off and wanted to put my head down next to the keyboard. I needed to leave and get some sleep before I could make any sense out of this.

Making sure that I didn't get a call on any systems issue, I logged off, closed the door, and went outside. There were lights on in the lodge, on the slopes, and in the parking lots. The resort was as bright as daylight. To make sure I didn't fall asleep while driving, I opened the window halfway and put the heater on high before I headed down the mountain.

# Chapter 39

I woke up on the spare cot when Stanley jumped up on my knees, whimpered, and licked my hands and face. It was nine o'clock.

"Hi, Stanley. How have you been?"

Ginny walked in and said, "Are you feeling rested?"

"Why didn't Ron wake me up for the shift change?"

"Don't be mad at Ron. When you walked in last night, you looked tired and mumbled something about them waiting so long. Ron pointed you to the cot, and you collapsed on it. Stanley followed and slept under it."

"Thanks for taking care of us. What's the news saying about the accident?"

"The resort doesn't think it's an accident. My police department insider said that it might have to do with PineTree."

"PineTree? How can they say that? The last time they disrupted the resort was the day the lift opened, and that was just chaining themselves to the guardrails and lying on the road."

"I know. That's just what I heard. Do you know something more than I do?"

"I don't think so. I guess we need to make sure everyone was safely rescued and hope that we don't lose the skiers to the other resorts. Stanley and I will go home for a little while, but I need to go back to the resort to check on the databases. Stanley can join me."

"You know he's welcome here."

"I know. Thanks."

When we got home, Stanley ran to his bed and started rolling around and growling. We had both missed home. After feeding Stanley and taking a shower, I sat down on the couch. I needed to return a few phone calls. I called my mom even though I knew she was probably enjoying lunch with her friends at the senior center. I left a message to tell her that everything was all right with me. I called Diane.

She said, "Mike, how are you? Since you didn't return my call, I assumed you were helping out on the rescue."

"I'm fine. Ron and I worked a six-hour shift last night, and I stayed a little longer to check the databases. I collapsed on a cot in the shop. I guess he felt sorry for me and didn't wake me up for the next shift. How are you and your parents?"

"I'm busy talking to the media—everyone from the local paper to Fox News. Dad is holding up well. He's been planning a bunch of meetings with our attorneys and the lift company. Mom and I are happy that Dad is taking charge and trying to fix this problem and salvage the ski season."

"I read an article in the *Elks Run Daily* that questioned whether this was an accident."

"The paper called me and took what I said a little out of context. All I said was that we are looking at all conceivable reasons for why this may have happened. I guess they assumed that I was saying that it wasn't an accident."

"What does your dad think caused it?"

"He said that it couldn't be a design fault or faulty operation. Brian agreed with him. What do you think?"

"To be honest, I don't know."

"Well, that's a first," she said with a giggle. "Depending upon our workload, can we see each other this weekend? I need some company."

"Sure. I need company too. I'll call you in a few days to see if we're still on."

"I need to go now. I will talk to you later. Take care. Love you. Bye."

I leaned back on the couch and closed my eyes. Joe Bunn and Brian Jones both had said that there wasn't a design flaw with the lift. That may be true. At the accident site, the towers fell over intact. I didn't see a break in any part of the towers.

*I drove up to the resort last fall and winter and saw the towers still being set in concrete with some very cold temperatures. The entire project was completed toward the end of December. That's when Diane and I rode the lift to the top. Could the cold temperatures have had something to do with all of this?*

The phone rang; it was Debbie.

"I got your message, and I'm sorry I didn't call you back."

"Please don't apologize. Last night on the news, I saw the rescue effort that was going on, and I knew you were involved in it. How are you doing?"

"Not too bad. Ron and I worked the first six hours of the rescue shift, and he went back this morning. I wanted to check the resort's computer system, and I stayed longer than I had anticipated. I came in late last night, and Ron didn't wake me up for the next shift."

"I don't think you know, but the attorneys for the resort are up a few floors from our offices. Through sources, I was led to believe that the lift might have been sabotaged."

I didn't say a word.

"Mike, are you there?"

"My sources here imply the same thing and—"

"And what?"

"I don't think it was sabotage."

"I know how you think, and you have been on the mark more than once. Would you like to talk to me about it?"

"I need to do a little more probing. For now, let me see what the investigation says caused the accident. I don't want to bore you with theories."

"Mike, your theories don't bore me."

"I need to hang up now, but you can call me anytime. How's Stanley?"

"Oh, he's going fine, especially with Ginny helping me out."

"She's the best. I'll talk with you soon. Bye."

I hung up and thought about Debbie, our marriage, and everything. *It's a little too overwhelming, but I know in my heart that she is one person I can fully trust.*

After hanging up, I got a call from my mom. She was glad that everything was fine with me. I mentioned that I had been speaking with Debbie, and she said that she hoped we could still be friends. Mom had always said that Debbie was good for me.

# Chapter 40

After another six hours of work by various teams, all the trapped skiers in the gondolas were safely rescued. It had been the first rescue of this size ever attempted; I hoped it would be the last. The skiers with the concussions were awake and doing well at St. Ambrose Memorial.

To maintain credibility with skiers, the resort gave every rescued skier a free lift pass for the rest of the season. Skiers who had lost equipment were given vouchers so they could replace it. I commended Diane for convincing her director that these actions would be in the best interests of the resort. Since the resort was reimbursing those who had lost or damaged their rental equipment, it was especially helpful for Ron and Ginny's shop. The accident hadn't really slowed down the skier visits. Many of the skiers decided it was only an accident and couldn't wait until the lift was working again. Unfortunately, I didn't think that was going to happen this season.

For two weeks after the collapse, there had been so much activity on the mountain. A special helicopter lifted the damaged towers off the mountain. A number of insurance agents and state investigators combed the area.

I was seeing a lot of database activity, and I was spending time increasing the log sizes of the backups. At least once a day, I'd been getting phone pages for database problems. That was all right because I was able to spend more time with Stanley. We'd been visiting the locker room and just hanging out together.

Diane called me and canceled our plans for the next weekend. Her dad needed to take a trip to the Sky Stream headquarters in California and had asked her to accompany him. I saw Joe Bunn almost every day, and he was preoccupied with his thoughts. He had asked me more than once how the computer system was going and whether I needed anything from him. I had asked Brian Jones on more than one occasion to delete his saved e-mail folder reports, and he was asking me how things were going. As far as I could remember, he had never gone out of his way to ask me how I was doing.

The snow had hit record levels for the season and had been phenomenal for the end of February. It snowed at least four inches every day. The town was using dump trucks to haul the snow away because there was nowhere to plow it in town. Colorado was a state with distinct contrasts. The high country had snow up to its rooftops, and Denver had little to none. People who were tired of seeing snow made a point of driving to Denver and spending a day in the city. After going to the museum or eating along Sixteenth Street, they bundled up and headed back to the mountains.

For three weeks after the accident, I kept hearing that the tower had been sabotaged. Diane was tight-lipped and said that the insurance company was still examining it. I thought she knew more, but it was all right because Joe Bunn had scheduled a news conference that would include law enforcement.

I told Cathy that I wasn't able to work that day, and I was not the only one. As important as the news conference was, Cathy made sure that there weren't many lessons scheduled. Ron was off, and we planned to drive to the resort together.

Ginny said that Stanley could spend time with her. She felt that it was important for us to go.

Ron and I didn't say much as we drove up the mountain. It started to snow as we pulled into a parking space.

"It looks like we'll have some good snow in the morning," Ron said.

I gave him a smile as we walked to the main lodge.

In the lodge, Joe Bunn was talking to Bob Trent and few other people I didn't recognize. I saw search and rescue, paramedics, and hospital people around the stage.

Diane was speaking to a few reporters nearby.

Joe Bunn stepped up to the microphone and said, "I want to say that I'm shocked as everyone who comes to enjoy the wonderful beauty of this resort and area about the accident that happened three weeks ago. I was very proud of our resort staff, search and rescue, our local and Denver hospitals, Colorado State Police, Chief Trent, and the Town of Elks Run for the way they responded to this disaster. They all did an exemplary job. There were 102 skiers rescued. Those skiers who were injured are doing well, and the prognostication is that they will all recover fully.

"During the past weeks, I have talked to many people. The local and state police, in conjunction with Sky Stream Lift Company, concluded the investigation by saying that the towers could only have collapsed because of some sort of sabotage. Because of a series of destruction by environmental groups to resorts and towns wanting to expand their areas, law enforcement contacted the FBI. The FBI examined the results of the police investigation, and they're conducting their own investigation. They haven't ruled out sabotage. I would like to introduce the special agent in charge of this investigation. Special Agent Jeff Peters will tell you more about the FBI investigation."

A man in a dark suit, a white shirt, and a striped tie approached the podium and opened a folder. "I'm Special Agent Jeff Peters, and I work at the Denver FBI field office. We received a call from the Colorado Bureau of Investigation three days after the towers collapsed. CBI's preliminary investigation said the towers fell because of tampering with the tower platforms. Because Elks Run Resort leases land from the Forrest Service and Bureau of Land Management, we reviewed their information and are conducting our own investigation. We have not ruled out sabotage.

"At this time, we are in the process of questioning Joe Crop. Mr. Crop is the regional director of PineTree. PineTree has been responsible for a number of disruptions at Elks Run and other resorts within Colorado, Utah, and Montana. We will keep the Colorado Bureau of Investigation and the local police informed about our investigation of Mr. Crop and PineTree. However, if any person believes that he or she knows anything of importance concerning this crime; please contact your local or state police and our office. I'll attempt to keep all parties informed about our investigation and its progress and have no other information to give you." Joe Bunn stepped up to the microphone and said, "Because the investigation is in progress, Special Agent Peters, local police, and CBI are not going to answer any questions from you. However, I can answer a few general questions."

The first question asked whether skiers were suing the resort for any of their injuries.

Politely, he said that he didn't know of any suits or whether the injured skiers had filed any. "Yesterday, I visited a skier who received a concussion. He was in very good spirits. He's hoping the towers can be repaired so that he can ski the back bowls."

A few people clapped in the crowd.

"I'll take one more question."

"Mr. Bunn, speaking of the Blue Sky lift, will it be able to become operational for the rest of the season?"

"I wish I could say that it would be, but with the weather being as cold as it was, the towers cannot be set. Hopefully, it will be operational for the summer season. I am sorry, but I need to end this conference. Thank you for coming." He and Jeff Peters left the room.

# Chapter 41

Diane and her father were walking toward the rear of the lodge.

"Mike, do you want to talk with Diane? I can wait."

"Thanks Ron, but it's okay. Let's just go." As we headed toward the front of the lodge, I was glad that they may have found a motive of why this happened, yet, I'm not sure if it's right.

"Mike, are you okay?" Ron asked.

"I guess I'm still tired. Maybe, I need more sleep."

"You're full of crap. We've been friends for a long time, and I know you. What's on your mind that doesn't add up?"

"Ron, I believe that this was a crime, but PineTree had nothing to do with it."

"Are you kidding? What do you know that the FBI doesn't? Did you see something or read something on the resort computers?"

"A little of both. Before I can say for sure, I need to drive back to the resort and check the databases again."

"If PineTree didn't sabotage the towers, who do you think did?"

"The resort did."

"Are you crazy? Why in the world would Elks Run want to damage its own lift? Was it for the insurance?"

"Maybe it was for greed, pride, or stupidity. I don't know, but I need to think about this a little more before I can say for sure. If my thinking is wrong, then it's wrong, and I'll accept it. But if the resort was behind this, then I guess I need to tell someone."

"You know how much we need these jobs, and you need to be right. I want you to know that you can run things by Ginny or me. I imagine Diane doesn't know about this."

"For the past week or so, I haven't seen Diane. I don't think she needed to hear what I think. Before this news conference, she all but said that it was sabotage."

"Have you spoken to Debbie?"

"I did say something to her, and she was open to anything else I may think of."

"Can you trust her?"

"I know I can."

When we walked into the shop, Ginny said, "How was the news conference? I guess your insider was right on the money."

"I can fill you in on it, but the FBI is questioning Joe Crop, the PineTree guy."

"You don't say," Ginny replied.

"Stanley and I are going back to the resort to do some work."

"I bought dinner for all of us. You sure you can't stay a little longer?"

"Not really. But can I certainly take it along with me," I said with a smile.

"Sure. Let me send you off with a bag for you and a bowl of food for Stanley."

Stanley perked his ears up and followed Ginny to the kitchen.

"Here you go, Mike." Ginny handed me the bags. "Thanks. I'll talk to you soon."

We headed out the door and made our way around large snow mounds to the truck.

# Chapter 42

The snow started to fall harder. As I drive through it, I was thinking about how to verify what I was thinking.

*Verify what? Maybe, I should just let this go. The FBI knows more than I do. Maybe I didn't see those anchor bolts. Maybe it was the angle, and what I saw was the branches of the trees that lined up with the top of the bent steel rods.*

I took a big breath and blew it out slowly. The snow wasn't plowed in this part of the parking lot. "Okay Stanley, let's walk through the snow. I'll save you if you get buried."

He started plowing through the snow with his ears dragging.

In the lobby, the receptionist was gathering her things to leave for the day.

"June, you may want to take it easy driving down."

"I will. Hi, Stanley, are you working with Dad tonight?"

"June, is anybody else here tonight?"

"Yes, I think Mr. Bunn and Mr. Jones are still here. I haven't seen them leave yet." Stanley and I settled in the computer room. I felt Stanley's head on my foot.

"Okay, Stanley. I'll feed you, and then I'll eat." I opened up a bag and poured his dry food in a bowl. Ginny had overdone it; the sesame chicken and pork fried rice were still warm. I broke up one of the chicken nuggets and sprinkled it on Stanley's food. "Here you go Stanley."

While eating, I started writing down what I want to prove—and how was I going to do it. I went back to the very beginning when I started with the resort.

*I remember giving the databases and the e-mail servers more space on a consistent basis. Yeah, there was a lot of the activity from Joe Bunn and Brian Jones. I am happy that Joe Bunn let me spend $8,000 to buy more data storage.*

While writing my plan, I began logging into the databases. Doing a quick check, I noticed a tremendous amount of activity.

*It's as if there is some program running in a loop and performing the same activity over and over. What's happening?*

Logging into a terminal O/S screen, I ran some cryptic commands and saw someone deleting data from the mountain report application. That someone was Brian Jones.

*Okay, what's he deleting? Let me think. I can do a comparison with what existed before. Yeah, I can build another database with the backup files just before Brian started deleting data from it. I had better check the e-mail servers. Same thing was happening here. But, within the e-mail servers, Brian Jones and Joe Bunn are deleting their e-mails. I can create another e-mail server just like the one I create for the databases.*

I leaned back in the chair and closed my eyes.

*All I wanted to do was get my consulting business off the ground and live in the mountains. I have that now, but why do I want start all over again? I should pack it up and stop being a computer forensics detective.*

I leaned forward and looked at the time. It was after five. I had been at it for a few hours, and Stanley was sound asleep on his bed. I reached for my iPhone to call Debbie, but then I stopped. I told myself that I needed to get more work done. Putting on my headphones, I reached down, turned on the cassette player, and started to listen to the music.

I created a third database and e-mail server from the backup files to a time before Brian and Joe started deleting the data. To be on the safe side, I went back to eight in the morning in case the FBI or anyone else wanted to look at reports or e-mails from the day of the tower crash since they may have plotted to do this before the news conference.

Two hours later, my eyes were hurting and Stanley was whimpering to go out. I felt good about the where I was and logged out of the databases and e-mail servers.

"Okay, Stanley, let's go home." He charged toward the door. I made sure that I turned off the cassette player and the lights, and I closed the door behind us. Walking up the stairs, I heard voices in the lobby. I felt as though I should stop in the stairwell, but Stanley didn't, and we continued walking.

Turning the corner, I saw Brian Jones and Joe Bunn. As soon as they saw me, they stopped talking.

I quickly said, "Brian, Mr. Bunn, how are things going for both of you?"

"Hello Mike and Stanley. Is everything all right with the computer system? You seem to working late tonight," Joe said.

"Oh, everything looks good. With the forecast for heavy snow, I wanted to make sure that I didn't need come in."

"That's good. We don't want to add that to our other problems. Drive safely."

"Thanks. You too."

Brian just smiled at us and didn't say a word. After I buttoned my coat and put on my hat and gloves, Stanley and I walked to the truck. Using my peripheral vision, I saw Joe and Brian talking in front of their cars. I started the truck and waited for the windshield to defrost. Driving to town, my gut feeling was that they were hiding something—and I would have loved to know what it was.

# Chapter 43

When my alarm rang, Stanley was up on his hind legs on the side of my bed and looking at me.

"Okay, okay. I'm getting up." I yawned and put on my sweats and jacket.

When I opened the garage door to let Stanley out, snow piled up against it fell into the garage. By the amount, I guessed it had snowed about four inches.

As Stanley made his way back into the garage, I swept the snow back outside and closed the garage door. When I said, "Let's eat," he charged up the stairs to the kitchen.

I turned on the TV and got our breakfasts. As big as this story was for Colorado's mountain area, I changed to a Denver channel. After listening to the weather and the gourmet chef, a report on Elks Run was next. The channel showed clips of the news conference. My ears perked up when I heard the reporter say that Joe Crop was the FBI's prime suspect. In less than a day, Joe Crop was questioned and was now the prime suspect.

I shut off the TV and finished my breakfast. Just then, the phone rang.

"I hope I didn't wake you," Diane said.

"No, Stanley and I are up and running."

"I'm so sorry that I wasn't able to call for the past two weeks," she said with a weary voice.

"There's no need to apologize to me. I know you and your family have been stressed."

"Thanks for your understanding. Dad was actually feeling better knowing that PineTree caused the collapse. So am I. With how many times I canceled our dates, I was wondering if we could see each other this weekend. That's if you want too."

I thought about the work I needed to do on the database and made up a lie. "Ron and I were thinking about having a guy's night out this weekend."

"Oh, I understand. Don't feel bad. Maybe we can plan something for next weekend?"

"Yes, that would be great. We may want to include some snowboarding in there."

"That would be great. It's been weeks, and I would love to get back on my snowboard," she said cheerfully.

"Okay, then, that's a date."

After hanging up the phone, I said, "Stanley, let's go spend another sunny day in the beautiful snow."

Stanley waddled to the garage.

# Chapter 44

Stanley and I walked in through the back door. "Good morning, Ginny. How are you doing this morning?"

"Great. How are you guys this morning?"

Stanley was wagged his tail and zoomed off to the back room.

"Is Ron here?" I asked.

"The last time I saw him, he was shaving. Tell me, why do guys take longer to shave their faces than we do shaving our legs, especially since we have more ground to cover?"

"Maybe Ron needs to be careful shaving around that monstrous mustache he's sporting."

Ron entered the room. "I know someone is talking about me because my nose is itching. What's Ginny saying about me now?"

"She just said how lucky she is to have you in her life," I said.

Ginny left for the front counter, and Ron pulled me aside. "Are you working today?"

"I called Cathy to say that I needed to work on the resort database. There was something odd happening last night. First, Brian Jones was doing a lot of deleting on the mountain report application. Then, Brian and Joe Bunn were deleting e-mails. I don't know what this all means, but I am trying to find out."

"You don't say," Ron said with a puzzled look. "If there are any e-mails that incriminate Joe or Brian, this will rock the resort. I don't want to see anything happen to you. Are you sure you want to go through with this?"

"There are too many what-ifs that I cannot answer. I don't understand why I'm doing it, but I am."

"I didn't say anything to Ginny. I don't want her to worry about you. If you need me, just call. I mean that."

"You bet I will." I said good-bye to Ginny and Stanley and left for the resort.

# Chapter 45

June noticed me in the lobby and said, "Mr. Bunn left me a note saying that I should ask you to see him if I saw you."

"Can you call Janet and ask if it's all right to see him now?"

She called and said I could go right up.

My mind raced as I walked up the stairs. I needed to stay sharp. Janet waved me in.

Joe said, "Since I haven't been able to talk to any of my staff in the past couple weeks, I decided to meet with them individually. Diane told me you spent time rescuing skiers from the cars. I want to thank you for a job well done."

"Mr. Bunn, there were many others too."

"I know. It was a hell of a job by everyone. How is the computer system holding up through all of this? I saw you staying late, and I am concerned that there are issues."

"I am just running through my normal checks on the system. Everything is functioning normally."

"The FBI believes that this was sabotage by PineTree, and I want to make sure you help them if they need any information off the resort database. Unless you officially receive a request from me or our attorney, Mr. Anthony Bell, no one should be given any data. Here is his card."

I came up with another lie. "Mr. Bunn, there's no need to worry. I'll help whenever possible, but I can only go back to a certain date because not all the e-mails are being saved. It takes too much space to save them."

"You don't say? Just give them what you can. You're the expert. You continue to do a great for the resort, and Diane and I appreciate it." He stood up, we shook hands, and I left.

*I must start looking at their e-mails, but I read somewhere that it's not legal. Maybe I can just glance over some of the e-mails just to satisfy my curiosity and to determine whether I should continue my detective work.*

I logged into the third e-mail server I created and went back four months. Glancing over Brian's sent e-mails, I read that a quite a number of them were sent to Joe Bunn and Sky Stream. I opened one sent to Joe Bunn just before the grand opening.

*Joe, I cleared all the huddles with the state, and we are a go for the opening. After reviewing the data and pictures I sent to Sky Stream, they said they didn't see any issues with Blue Sky on their end. I guess it's too late to turn back. I was hoping for sunny weather for the next month with just limited amount of snow. Brian.*

*I wonder what he means by saying it's too late to turn back now.*

Joe Bunn had sent a reply a few minutes later.

*Brian, I don't need you to get cold feet; it's too late to turn back. You need to focus on the lift by monitoring all the data 24/7. Make sure you don't forget to pick up the Sky Stream rep at the airport. I don't want any surprises at this point. Joe.*

*Interesting, a Sky Stream rep was here when the towers collapsed. It seems his presence didn't really help, did it? All right, I can't get cynical and need to focus. Let me pull up an e-mail after the collapse. This one looks interesting.*

*Did you get them? You need to find them before anyone else does. Make sure search and rescue doesn't get in that area before you do. Come and see me when you come down.*

*What would Brian have to find up there?*

I leaned back in the chair and looked up at the ceiling. The ceiling lights must have caused a light bulb to go off in my head, and I thought about what I had seen at the towers.

*The missing bolts—that had to be it. Brian must have taken them off the towers. They were there before Brian reached tower fourteen, and after he left, they were gone. And I thought my eyes were deceiving me. I wonder if Brian was going to keep them or already planted them on Joe Crop. I need to talk to someone.*

# Chapter 46

"Debbie, I'm sorry if I'm calling you too late, but I really need to talk to you."

"It's eleven o'clock, and I have to defend an important client in court at nine, but I'll charge you half-price," she said with a chuckle. "By the way, weren't we trying to have dinner one of these weekends—or maybe you thought it wasn't worth it?"

"Believe me; I want us to have that planned dinner."

"Next year?" There was silence from both of us. "I'm sorry. That wasn't kind."

"No. I was wrong in not calling you back, but I remember telling you that I needed to do more probing into the accident."

"This sounds serious. I'm all ears."

I told her everything, and Debbie listened intently. "Mike, have you spoken to anyone else besides Ron and Ginny?"

I was glad that Debbie considered them friends and knew whatever I told them was confidential. "I talked to no one else besides Ron, and he didn't say anything to Ginny."

"When you told me that you needed to look into this accident a little more, I expected the worst."

*That's good. She hasn't forgotten how I think.*

"I would think a good start would be to find those bolts from the towers. As far as those emails you read, the only way the law enforcement can read them would be with a court order. That's if they surmise if a crime had been committed. Mike, this is getting serious, and I don't want to see you get hurt. I really don't."

I felt a rush of passion toward her, thinking of the many times we had held each other and made love. "Debbie, I don't want you to get hurt either. I may need your help as my attorney or by referring me to someone else."

"Mike, since we are legally divorced, there isn't a reason why I couldn't represent you. I guess there are advantages. Did you plan this whole thing so you could test my law skills?"

"Sure—and this was a good way for us to get together for lunch too."

"Touché. I don't know what you should do next."

"I know. It would be ideal if I could find those bolts. I can't go to the police to tell them that I read incriminating e-mails. And I don't know why the FBI arrested Joe Crop unless they found some incriminating evidence, possibly some tower parts or the bolts. I'll ask Ginny to talk to her contact within the police department. Maybe I can get more information."

"I'll try to find out a little more from the resort's insurance adjuster. I think he wants to ask me out."

*That caught me off guard.*

"Mike, are you there? You aren't jealous?"

"No, well, to be honest, I wasn't expecting that one."

"There is no way I would ever go out with him. He's not my type, but it's nice to know that you may still be a little jealous. I'll find that information out another way and give you a call. Please stay safe. If you need me, call me on my cell—no matter what time—and I'll get back to you. I wouldn't mind if we see each other before our official date."

"I'm glad that you haven't lost your sense of humor."

"And I'm glad that you haven't lost your sense of integrity and fairness. By the way, how is Stanley taking all of this?"

"I can't ask him because he's sleeping."

We both laughed.

"Deb, thanks for the chat. We both need to get some sleep. Goodnight."

"Goodnight. Please take care. I'll talk to you soon."

# Chapter 47

It felt good to work with an intermediate snowboard class. Talking to the students and riding some good terrain took my mind off the fact that the resort brought fun and danger to many people.

After the class, I headed to the main lodge for lunch. While waiting in the buffet line, I felt a shove from a tray in my back.

Diane said, "Are you avoiding me?"

"No. What makes you say that?"

We paid for our lunches and sat down on the outside veranda.

"I thought we were going to get together last weekend. You were supposed to call me."

"I'm really sorry. I should have called you. Since the lift accident, I haven't been feeling well mentally or physically."

"I know. I'm sorry I used that tone of voice with you. My parents have been on edge since it happened, and I needed something to get me back to normal. I was hoping that you would be able to help me feel normal again."

*Did she want to tell me something that her parents said that made her uncomfortable?*

"Diane, let's go boarding tomorrow. I think it will help both of us."

"I have some reports to complete, but they can wait. Let's do it. What time?"

"Let's shoot for ten. We'll miss the powder, but we may beat the lines."

"Don't talk about powder because I probably forgot how to ride in it. Ten is great. I need to get going. Thanks a lot." She touched my hand and kissed me on the cheek.

I watched her leave, and then I stared out over the slopes with the sun in my face. I thought back in time in seeing the smiles on my parents' faces as I skied by or when Debbie and I got married. It would nice to see my mom smile again.

# Chapter 48

The morning started with snow, but by the time Diane and I took our first run, the sun was shining brightly. It felt like years since we had boarded together.

After a couple of good runs, we headed to the main lodge.

"That was great. I hope I didn't embarrass you or myself."

"I think you did great, and you'll only get better," I said as we ordered breaded clams and beer. "How are your mom and dad doing?"

"Dad got a call from the insurance company. They are sending the resort a check for the towers. Dad said that Brian Jones will coordinate the rebuilding this spring. Everything should be up and running for the summer season."

"That's great."

"Is there something wrong?"

"I just don't know whether PineTree could have sabotaged the towers."

"I don't think I'm hearing you correctly. You're saying that you don't believe that PineTree committed the sabotage. How could you? The FBI and everyone else involved in this whole mess arrested the ringleader. This same person caused traffic disruptions at the resort, outbursts at the town meetings, and possibly other crimes that we don't know of. Apparently, the FBI did because he's their prime suspect. They also found incriminating evidence in his car. What could you possibly know that FBI doesn't?"

"I don't know any more than you do, but I met Joe Crop at a town meeting, and he seemed to be a levelheaded guy. He was trying to present his views, which he had a right to do."

"I thought you were the real deal, a strong, athletic, and levelheaded guy. My dad thought so too—that's why he gave you the consulting job with the resort. How could you think that way? I'm leaving. Don't bother calling me." She threw down her napkin and walked away.

*Well, that certainly went well. I thought I got the resort contract because of my computer skills, not because of how much I could lift at the gym. Why the hell did I say that? I know I'll have a job in the morning, but I don't know about next year.*

# Chapter 49

In the morning, I didn't feel like showing my face at the resort. For all I knew, Diane told her Dad what I said, which could make working conditions a little uncomfortable.

The phone rang, and Ginny said, "How are you and Stanley doing this morning?"

"It's one of those I-don't-want-to-work days."

"I'm sorry to hear that, but Ron asked me to find out what the FBI could have on Joe Crop. I asked my inside person; apparently, they found tower bolts in his car. He said in a statement that he doesn't lock his car all the time, and anyone could have put it in his car."

"Diane alluded to some incriminating evidence yesterday, but I bet I know who put that bolt in his car. Unfortunately, I can't prove it."

"Ron told me what you think may have happened; to be honest, I don't believe it. However, we both think that it's a possibility and are worried about you."

"I know I can count on you. By the way, I talked to Debbie about all of this, and it's nice to have her support."

"That must mean loads to you."

"It does. You're super for getting this information for me."

"If there's anything else you need from us, let us know."

"Thanks. See you this afternoon."

I checked my work calendar and counted twenty days that I had worked this season. That meant that I had completed my obligation as a part-time instructor. The resort couldn't fire me because of that.

*Why am I getting paranoid? I don't think Diane said anything to her dad. Come on, I need to get a grip on myself.*

"Stanley, I need to work one more day on the slope for good measure—and then we can spend more time together." I got on the floor and started roughhousing with him.

After dropping off Stanley with Ginny, I stopped by the Coffee Mug Café. "Hi Jeff, can I have a large coffee and room for cream?"

"Mike, I haven't seen you for a while. Are you still working for the resort?" he said as he handed me the coffee.

"Yeah, still there, just been busy."

The forecast called for snow in the afternoon. True to form, it started as I drove to the resort. I parked the truck and went to find Cathy.

As usual, she was at the instructors' meeting area at the Stairwell lift. She thanked me for checking in because she couldn't get anyone to take a beginning class. I wondered why.

The class was uneventful, and my back hurt a little from picking up half the class.

Walking to the lockers, John Swan yelled, "Mike, it's good to see you. How are things going for you? I haven't seen you since we worked on getting the skiers down from the lift."

"John, it's good to see you too. I've been working more on the computer side than the slope side. I just finished a beginner's class, and my back is aching. Cathy was kind to me. If I get an advanced class, somebody will need to carry me down."

"You need to get out there more often, but I've got the remedy. A few of us are going to TT's right after we change. You're welcome to join us."

*That's exactly what the doctor ordered.* "I'll be there. It'll be nice to relax."

I changed quickly and took off for the computer room. I needed to make sure that all my stealth work was still there. In the administrative lobby, I saw a few men get out of an Elks Run police car and an unmarked police car. Some of them were detectives or FBI because I saw suits under their overcoats.

Chief Bob Trent said hi to me as he and the other men walked up stairs. I presumed they were meeting with Joe Bunn. As I checked the computer system, my heart and mind raced. *Are they going to ask me questions? Will they ask for e-mails? Am I going to mention the e-mails that I found? Should I tell them what I found? Should I call Debbie?*

It went on and on in my head. I closed my eyes, took a deep breath, and let it out slowly. That helped. I waited for a call from Joe Bunn or a knock on my door. I got no call or knock. Since everything was the same as I left it, I logged off and headed for TT's.

# Chapter 50

TT's was crowded with skiers and resort employees.

John said, "The way everyone greeted you made it seem as though they hadn't seen you in years," he said with a smile.

"Yeah, it feels that way. Most asked me about Stanley. But I'm not complaining. It feels good to be out for a while." I ordered a Coors light. "Hey, where's everyone else?"

"I don't know, but they may be coming a little later."

"Since I haven't seen you out on the slopes, I assume that you have been really busy doing your computer thing. Has that been going well for you?"

"Yes, it's been good and busy for me. I'm also trying to stop by other small businesses in town to possibly land other work. If you don't mind, here are a few of my business cards for your friends in town or even in Denver." I reached for my wallet and took a few out.

"That's no problem. I'm glad to help you out."

"How's school going for you? Aren't you going to finish your fourth year soon? Do you have any thoughts about what you would like to do when you graduate?"

"I don't know, but I've been thinking about working for the EPA. I could make a difference."

"That's noble of you, but do you think you could put up with all the bureaucratic crap? Government agencies could be brutal environments."

"I thought about that, but I need to start somewhere. What better way to start than learning how the government operates—or maybe how it doesn't?"

We ordered another round.

"Not to change the subject, but I believe the FBI arrested the wrong person. There is no possible way that Joe Crop could have caused those towers to collapse. Yes, he was vocal about many environmental issues and stopped traffic with his convictions, but there's no way he would hurt other people. He's an intellectual. He would rather browbeat you in an environmental argument than lift a finger to hurt you."

"John, I think I believe you."

"You do? Then, what do you think happened?"

"I don't know, but when was the last time you spoke to Joe?"

"It was the day before the lift collapsed. He said that he was going to visit his sister in Colorado Springs the day the lift collapsed."

"Maybe some of his PineTree friends did it."

"Mike, you've got to kidding. Most of his people don't ski, board, or snowshoe. They like the summer weather. You won't find them out in cold weather unless they have to be. If you met them, you would agree that they don't have the know-how or desire to sabotage the towers."

"Did you say anything to Chief Trent about Joe Crop going to see his sister on the day of the tower collapse?"

"I did, and I signed a written statement. If he didn't do it, then who did? Was it something not under anyone's control?"

"Maybe it was a little of both." I slapped him on his shoulder.

"It's getting late, Mike. I'm going to head out now. Are you staying?"

"I think I'll finish my beer and leave shortly. It looks like we're in for a little more snow tonight." I looked out the windows. "Be careful driving."

"You too. And I hope to see you on the slopes before the season ends." He finished his beer and walked out the front door.

It felt good to go to TT's and see John and the others. At least I knew of one other person who thought PineTree didn't sabotage the towers. I didn't want to see Diane; it had been a week or two since our unfriendly discussion. I didn't blame her because I would probably stand up for my father in the same matter.

I left a tip for the bartender, put on my coat, and started out for the door. The snow hitting my face felt good. Making my way over recently plowed snow, I noticed someone having a difficult time walking in the parking lot. It seemed that this person was bouncing from car to car like the ball in a pinball machine. It could be suicidal for anyone to drive in this weather, especially someone who could hardly stand up.

I shuffled a little faster through the snow to catch up. I noticed the person had on the Elks Run parka worn by management. "Hey, are you feeling okay." I tapped the person on the shoulder.

To my surprise, it was Brian Jones. "Oh, hi. Who are you?" he slurred.

"Brian, do you know me? I'm Mike Doyle."

He looked at me with glazed eyes as he swayed from side to side. "Mike? Mike Doyle? What time is it? I need to get home. Where was my truck?" He started looking for his keys and fumbled through the jacket pockets.

"Brian, what kind of truck do you drive?" I steadied him against the nearest car.

"Ford. Ford truck. A big green one," he said.

*Great.* I leaned him against a car, told him to stay put, and looked around for the truck. Under an overhead light pole, I saw a barely discernible truck under the snow.

After couple minutes of fishing through his pockets, I found the keys. "Okay, Brian, let's see if we can make it to the truck." I grabbed his arm, and we made our way to the truck.

*What am I supposed to do when I get there? I can't leave him in the truck to sleep it off or have him drive home. It's too cold, and he's too drunk.*

Leaning him against the truck, I unlocked the door. "Brian, I think you need to get into your truck before you start suffering from hypothermia. You won't be able to drive tonight. Okay?"

"I know. I know, but if you can get me to the condo, I can sleep it off."

"Brian, where's your condo?"

*I'm in for a long night.*

"Oh, it's here in Elks Run. The resort owns it." I shook him again. "The resort owns it."

"Brian, where is it? Can you tell me where it is?"

"Yeah, 112 Elks Run Bull, no Boulevard. The keys are in the glove compartment. It's only a few blocks from here."

I knew it well because Diane lived two streets away. I decided to drive him and walk back to my truck. The walk would be good for me. Stepping on the running board, I pulled him into the back seat.

When I pulled out the keys from the glove compartment, it had the address on the key ring with his name on it. I didn't know the staff had that perk. I just hoped no one else was using it. Pulling up to the closed gate, I entered the numbers that I read off the key ring. That worked. In 112, I didn't see any lights on, and I decided to check it out before I dragged Brian in the door.

Knocking on the door, I heard no response. Slowly, I opened the door with the key and turned the lights on. Quickly, I did a search of the bedrooms and bathroom. It was a fully furnished two-bedroom unit, and no one was there. It took me a good five minutes to get Brian into the condo. I was glad it was on the first floor. I decided on the nearest bedroom and dropped Brian on the bed. He murmured that he needed his clothing bag and shoes from the truck. I think he said that it was in the back of the pickup bed.

As I unlocked the pickup bed cover and pushed it up, a light went on. I saw the clothing bag under a green wool blanket. Uncovering the bag, I saw a box behind it. Maybe his shoes were in it because they weren't in the clothing bag. Opening the box flap, I stared in the box. It may have been a few seconds, but I thought it was a few minutes.

What I saw resembled the tower bolts from the top of the concrete bases. I picked one up and looked at it. It was dark silver, quite heavy, and felt sharp. My mind went blank. I looked deeper in the box to see how many more were in there. I counted ten. I knew that there were six anchor bolts for each tower. Two were missing. I bet the FBI found them in Joe Crop's car. How stupid could he be hiding them in his truck. *Now what?*

I decided to hide one of them on the top of the rear tire. I'd take it with me when I left. I closed the box the same way I found it and locked the cover. Carrying the clothing bag and shoes back to the condo, I put them in the bedroom closet. So he could see it, I left the closet doors open. I poured a glass of water from the faucet and sat down at the kitchen counter. I had the smoking gun. Joe Crop could really be innocent.

I wanted to call Debbie, but I knew it wouldn't be wise to do it from there. I walked into the bedroom, and Brian was fast asleep. I saw an extra blanket in the closet and covered him. I zipped up my jacket and left, locking the door behind me.

# Chapter 51

After picking up Stanley, it took me some time to get to asleep. My mind couldn't stop racing. I woke up to Stanley whimpering in my face as he stretched himself to stand up on the side of the bed.

"Okay, Stanley, let's get some breakfast."

He ran into the kitchen.

I felt drugged from the lack of sleep. I wouldn't say anything to Ron or Ginny about the bolts because I needed to talk to Debbie first. As I sat down for breakfast, the phone rang. It startled both of us.

"I'm sorry to call you so early, but I need all the instructors I can get. Until this morning, I didn't know we were getting two high school buses from Denver. I'll need you at ten."

"No problem, Cathy. I need to stop by the bank when it opens at nine, but I should be ready to go at ten."

Cathy couldn't thank me enough.

I loaded Stanley in the car and dropped him off with Ginny. I didn't say anything to Ginny or Ron because I didn't want them to get involved.

At the bank, I asked for my safe deposit box. Signing the log and showing my license, I carried the square box to an empty room and closed the door behind me. Opening my backpack, I took out the tower bolt. Before putting it in the box, I looked at it closely. The bolt looked to be about four inches thick and weighed a couple of pounds. I noticed that a discolored crack appeared on the surface of the bolt for about an inch with a little gap that disappeared into the metal.

Before putting it in the box, I checked the other papers. There was a deed to the townhouse, our original marriage license, and old savings bonds. I closed the deposit box and gave it back to the clerk. She probably thought I had put a gold bullion bar in it. Putting the key in my wallet, I drove to the resort.

It was great to help Cathy out after all she had done for me. Even if that meant taking a class of kids who thought riding a skateboard was the same as riding a snowboard. I think the difference was friction, and they didn't find it on the snow. At least I got get a little more respect after the lesson.

While I walked back to change my clothes, I called Debbie. She wasn't available, and I didn't bother leaving a message on her work phone. I called her cell phone and left a message.

*I really need to talk to her. If Brian Jones figured out that one of the bolts was missing, how will he track it down? Even if he was drunk, I think I will be in his sights.*

Before I reached the locker door, Diane walked up to me with a pair of skis. She was with another instructor. I hadn't seen her since our shaky lunch. She said, "I went out for a lesson with Kevin. I'm trying to sharpen up my skiing skills. Kevin was really good."

"Yes. "He's the best." I smiled at him. "I hope everything is going well for you. It's good to see you." She and Kevin walked away.

*I can't blame her. I didn't call. I am too busy trying to be a detective.*

As I finished changing my clothes, Ron said, "Mike, were have you been? We haven't seen you in days. Are you all right?"

"Sorry. I've been busy. Cathy needed help on the slopes and I've been working on the computer system, but it's no excuse. I should have kept in touch."

"Are you finished for today?"

"I am, and it'll be good to help Ginny out. She has had her share of long hours, and I need to look at our inventory. What are you up to?"

"I thought about going to TT's or Bob's Place tonight. However, I need to check whether the resort pool team needs a replacement player because I did volunteer to help out. If I get out of here a little late, can I drop Stanley off?"

"You know that's not a problem. If you need a ride home from either place, give us a call."

"Don't feel bad about Diane seeing Kevin. Your principles are different. Believe me. That's what important."

"How long have you known?"

"Only a few weeks, but you know how Kevin operates. He started bragging to other instructors that he was dating Diane. That's how I found out. I thought you knew."

"No. I didn't, but it's all right," I said. It hurt a little, but that is what happens in the ski resort world. "I'm going to pick Stanley up and will come back to do some work here."

"Tell Ginny I'll be home soon. I need to pick up a few supplies."

As I reached the truck, my cell phone rang.

Debbie said, "Sorry I couldn't call you sooner, but you sounded a little stressed. Are you all right?"

"Deb, I have a bolt from the ski lift tower."

She was silent for a few seconds. "How did you find it?"

I explained everything.

"Have you told anyone?"

"No—not even Ron or Ginny."

"You may need a lawyer."

"I know, and I want the best. I would like to hire you."

"Okay, for a dollar retainer, you got a deal."

"All kidding aside, you need to stay safe. How about letting me talk to the ADA who's working this case and present him with this information. I'll do it tomorrow morning and will call you back as soon as I finish speaking to him. Then we can decide what the next step is."

I hadn't heard the word *we* in the same sentence for eight months, and it sounded different.

"Sure, I'll take care of myself and wait until you call tomorrow." I felt relieved that I had done the right thing—and Debbie was on my side.

# Chapter 52

I picked up Stanley and reminded Ginny about where Ron was going before he came home.

I said, "After a few hours at work and feeding him at home, I'll be dropping him off again. I'll be filling in for another pool player on the resort team. I told them I was a little rusty, but I guess that they needed a body. It might take my mind off of what has been happening to me."

Stanley and I made our way through the snow to the administrative building. I noticed that there were an unusual number of cars in the parking lot. Stanley shook the snow off his back as we walked to the computer room.

The room was cool, but I put on the little heater under the desk to keep my feet warm.

Stanley jumped on his bed.

I put on my earphones, pressed the forward button to listen to music on the cassette player on his bed. I logged on to the databases and checked whether they were still in sync, including the third one I had created. They were. It was important because someone might need to see the deleted data from the files. All the e-mail servers were working fine, including the third one I created.

*That's funny. I don't see the e-mail server space being used as quickly as in the past. Maybe Brian and Joe stopped sending e-mails to each other. I wonder why.*

Stanley raised his head, sat up, and barked once, as I pushed my chair away from the desk and looked at him. He was looking at the door.

"What is it, Stanley?"

I took off the earphones and heard a knock on the door. I opened the door.

Brian said, "May I come in?"

"Sure. I'm sorry, but I haven't had a visitor this season, and I was surprised by your knock. That's all."

"Sure, I understand. I wanted to thank you for taking care of me a couple days ago. I guess I was drunk, and driving was out if the question."

"Oh, that wasn't a problem. I'm glad that I was there and that the resort had a place so near for you. That was convenient."

"Yes, it was." His tone of voice changed. "Mike, when you got my clothes out of the back of my truck, did you by any chance take anything out of the box where my shoes were?"

"No. I just took your shoes out of the box. It was dark, and I had to feel for them. Why? Is there something missing?"

"Yes. There is something missing, and I think you know what it is. It would be healthy for you to return that missing item to me." He looked scary and downright dangerous. "It's important for the resort that the missing item be found. I wouldn't want anyone—especially you—to get hurt over it."

I needed to say something so he wouldn't know I had it. "Brian, I don't know why you're threatening me because I don't know what the hell you are talking about." I put my right foot back to give me some leverage if he took a swing or pushed me back.

"Don't give me that shit. You know what the hell I am talking about. There's a bolt missing, which you took from my truck. You need give it back to me—or losing your job at the resort will be the least of your problems." He pointed his finger about three inches from my face.

"Are you threatening me, Brian?"

"Again, for your health, you need to return that bolt to me today. I'll leave my office door open and the top drawer too. I need to see it tonight. I think you're a smart guy, and I think I've made my point clear to you." His face was red as he turned toward the door and slammed it behind him.

My heart was racing as I slowly sat down in my chair. Stanley licked my hand. His face looked concerned; he knew that Brian wasn't being friendly.

# Chapter 53

I left the building with Stanley, and I looked around for Brian's truck. I didn't see it, and I didn't know if that was a good thing.

*Should I go to the bank before it closes and get the bolt? Will I be able to live with knowing that this could send an innocent person to jail? Will he try to follow me home? Heck, he probably knows where I live anyway.*

I had to be at Bob's Place by 7:30. I dropped Stanley off and didn't mention anything to Ron and Ginny. Maybe, that was a mistake.

I said, "I'll try not to make a fool of myself playing pool. If I do, I'll pick up Stanley a little earlier."

We all laughed as I got on my knees and gave Stanley a big hug. Driving to Bob's, my mind traveled from the music on the radio to Brian's threat. I looked in the rearview mirror more than a few times.

Before I knew it, I was at Bob's Place. Because of the pool tournament, the parking lot was crowded. I couldn't find a level spot, and I parked halfway up a snow mound. I felt like an astronaut pulling myself out of the space shuttle and then tumbling backwards. It was very good reason to only have one—and no more than two—beers because I'd never get back into my truck.

The team had three guys and two gals that I had seen at the resort, but I didn't know their names. We all introduced ourselves. I changed my cue stick a few times, thinking that it affected my playing.

*I have to face the fact that I stink. It could be my nerves. Okay, I need to relax so I don't make a complete fool of myself.*

Either my team or the other one were all drunk because I started playing better. I even won two games for the team. After the matches, we all sat around and watching the Avalanche beat the Coyotes in Arizona.

We had a good time. It had been months since I had laughed and eaten so many shelled peanuts in one sitting.

It was getting late, and everyone started to leave around eleven. The final surprise was when I became the team's best replacement player because we won the game. Laughing and thanking them for this great opportunity, I said good-bye to Bob and headed for my car.

Climbing up the mound of frozen snow wasn't easy, but I was able to pull myself in my bucket seat. Since I couldn't scrape my windshield, I ran the engine to defrost the windshield. I took a left on Route 91 and headed toward I-70. As soon as I turned on 91, another car appeared behind me.

*The car just appeared out of nowhere. I need to drive carefully because the road is very slippery. The snowplows don't come through here as often as on the other roads. The car behind me is getting closer, and I'm getting a little uncomfortable. What's this guy doing? The headlights seem to be in my backseat. That car or truck is bigger than mine. There aren't any shoulder pull-offs until I get closer to I-70. There's just a big drop off. Great. Even if I slow down or speed up, the guy is still behind me. I know I can make it.*

Suddenly, it felt as though my car had a jet engine. The truck hit my rear bumper a couple of times. I reached for my phone and tried to dial 911. Things started happening fast. I needed to control my truck as the rear end started to skid to the left. I dropped the phone and turned my wheel quickly to the right to stop the skid. It was too late. My car spun around twice. I let go of the wheel and looked at the oncoming headlights and trees. I was thrown to my right, whipped to the left, bounced off a guardrail, and braced myself for the bottom of Blue River Gulch. That's when my memory went blank.

# Chapter 54

When I opened my eyes, I saw a soft glare of light shining off the glass in another room.

A nurse leaned over the gurney and said, "Hi, Mr. Doyle. My name is Nancy. Can you hear me? How are you feeling? You're in the ER at St. Ambrose's."

I didn't feel anything until she asked me. "I feel a little pain all over. Is that a good thing?"

"Excellent. You should be a doctor. Speaking of doctors, here's Dr. Hanes."

"Mike, I couldn't help but overhear that you're feeling a little pain all over. Is that right? I think the last time we saw each other was at the lift accident." He checked my pulse, blood pressure, and eyes. Then, he did a pressure test on my toes, feet, arms, and hands. "Since the paramedics found you in a ditch and the steering wheel airbag deployed, I made sure that we ran an MRI of your brain. It seems that you might have suffered a mild concussion because you were unconscious in your vehicle, but everything in the MRI looked normal. You were very lucky. Have you ever had a concussion?"

"No, I haven't, but would I remember it?" I answered with a little smile.

"Nancy, you were right. Mike should have been a doctor." He smiled back at me. "The MRI showed no internal bleeding." He asked me the date, where was I born, my address, and whether I could repeat a series of numbers.

Even though I was slow in my responses, my answers were correct. I passed the test.

"The X-rays show that you don't have any broken bones. We found some contusions on your face and arms. We need to keep you here for a few more hours. You'll need to call a chauffeur to take you home. Do you have anybody in mind?"

"Yes. Can someone call Ron or Ginny Gustaff for me?"

"Sure. We'll give them a call. I'm going to leave the intravenous saline connected until that bag drains completely. The saline solution is mixed with some antibiotics and a painkiller. The nurse will give you instructions for what to do for the next couple of days and a prescription for pain medication. You'll need to visit your family doctor for a follow-up appointment next week. You don't have to take a painkiller every few hours; just take it when you need it. If you start vomiting, feel nauseous or dizzy, or have blurred vision, call the number on the release instructions immediately. Okay?"

"Yes. Thanks, Doc."

He turned and left the room.

I must have fallen asleep because the next thing I heard was Ginny saying, "Mike, how are you?" She looked very concerned look.

Ron said, "Do you want to stay with us or go home?"

"Home please."

We all had a laugh. "Mike, your truck is at Fred's Garage."

"Did you get to see it?"

"Yes. Except for replacing most of the left side, it looks to be in good shape. I don't know the condition of the engine or drive train"

"What about the rear bumper? How does it look?"

"I saw dents in it, but you must have had those before. Didn't you?"

"No. I didn't. Someone tried to push me off the road in Blue River Gulch."

"Mike, is there something you aren't telling us?"

"Yes, but I made that choice so that you wouldn't be hurt."

"Is this something that has to do with the resort?" Ron asked with a little fear in his eyes.

"Can we talk about this tomorrow? Right now, I need to get some rest at home."

After the saline was finished, the nurse went over my release with Ron and Ginny.

"Mike, we'll be waiting outside."

As I slowly finished getting dressed, Chief Bob Trent walked into the room. "The paramedics reported that they didn't smell much alcohol on your breath. I did check with Bob, and he said you had two beers and a lot of peanuts. Your team kept a tab, and you're the only one that had Coors Light. Did you lose control on the ice?"

"No, Chief. Someone got behind me, hit my bumper a few times, and put me in a spin."

He stopped writing and pulled up a chair. "I didn't check your car for rear damage, but I will in the morning. Why do think someone wanted to spin you off the road? Someone may have lost control and hit your car. It may very well been an accident."

"I know. Can we talk about this tomorrow? I don't feel well and need to rest."

"Sure. I'll go over my notes with the state police. I can come to your house so you can finish writing your statement—or you can stop by and see me when you are up to it. Let me get Ron and Ginny back in here."

He walked out and talked to Ron and Ginny in the corridor.

Ron came back inside and said, "You told him?"

"Yes. He will know a lot more before this week ends. And so will you."

After the nurse released me, we headed home.

# Chapter 55

I woke up with pain all over. No matter how I tried to position myself, I hurt. I didn't know where Stanley could be since the bedroom door was closed.

Rolling over to my right side, I gently put my feet on the floor and pushed myself up. I put my bathrobe on and opened the door.

Stanley was on the floor, but he ran toward me. Ron jumped between us and told Stanley not to jump on me. "You didn't look good, and I decided to stay over to make sure you were okay. I started breakfast for us, and it should be ready soon. Do you think you can eat a little this morning? I already fed Stanley."

"Thanks a bunch. I don't remember much from yesterday, but I will try some breakfast."

"Chief Trent said that you told him that you don't believe it was an accident. Is this true?"

"I didn't want to get you guys involved with all of my speculations about whether the tower collapse was an accident or sabotage. After what happened to me last night, I can say that it wasn't sabotage; it was resort negligence. It was the resort attempting to put the blame on someone else. They chose Joe Crop. The only other person that I confided in was Debbie; I asked her to be my attorney."

"Holy crap, Mike. This is pretty serious. Ginny and I were thinking that you were depressed about Diane and your divorce. We didn't know. Do you think that whoever tried to steer you down the gulch was part of this cover-up?"

"I think so. I don't want to tell you anymore because you guys are my friends, but rest assured that this will cause Elks Run to fall or survive. I hope the latter."

"Are you saying that we might have to look for jobs at another resort? It's a good thing that we didn't burn any bridges behind us," he said with a smile.

"I don't know, but we have been known to move from resort to resort. Maybe it's time for a change," I said with a bigger smile.

"If we can help in any way, let us know. You can always count on us."

"I know I can."

"Ginny called Debbie on your accident."

"That's fine. Thanks for taking care of me. I'll be okay."

He gave me a big hug.

After calling my doctor, I set up an appointment with my insurance agent.

Ron offered to drive me.

As I sat down to eat my breakfast, the phone rang.

Debbie said, "Ginny called me. Are you all right? What in the world happened? Did you hit an ice patch?"

"I'm all right. Ron spent the night here. I needed to tell him that I thought arresting Joe Crop was a cover-up for the resort. I said that you would be helping me talk to someone in Denver about my suspicions."

"I said the same thing to Ginny. As a good friend, I think she was owed that."

"I was pushed off the road, and I think it was Brian Jones. I didn't return the bolt to him, and he was pissed. I told Chief Trent that I thought someone hit my bumper a few times. It was a large truck that I thought I saw in our parking lot. He said he was going to look at my car and the spot where I went off the road. I think I need to talk to someone. The sooner, the better."

"I agree. That's why we have a meeting with US Assistant District Attorney Jack Evans on Wednesday morning. Do you think you can stay out of trouble for the next day?"

"I'll try, but you know me."

"In case you're wondering, I am proud of what you are doing."

I was at a loss for words. "I need to visit the garage and see the damage on the truck. I think Chief Trent wants a statement from me. Should I mention anything to him?"

"I wouldn't. Just say that you'll be meeting with Jack Evans. Do you think you're up for it? If you are, can you bring the bolt? Do you want me to pick you up?"

"I think Ron can drive me. I'll be there."

"You be well—and take care of Stanley."

"I will. Thanks for helping me."

I swallowed a pain bill, and the phone rang. I picked up the phone.

Diane said, "I heard you were involved in an accident. Are you all right?"

"I'm doing fine. Just a little pain, but I should survive. Thanks for the call."

"Where did you skid off the road?"

"At Blue River Gulch."

"Did you tell Chief Trent that you thought Brian Jones pushed you off the road?"

"I said that I *think* someone pushed me off the road, either intentionally or by accident, but I didn't know who."

"He came by to question Brian today and asked to see his truck. Are you okay? First, you don't think Joe Crop caused the collapse—and now you're accusing Brian Jones of pushing you off the road?"

I was angry, but I didn't want to show it. "I'm not feeling well. Can we talk about it when I feel better?"

"I don't think so. I think you need help, and I can't help you. Maybe a psychiatrist can." She hung up.

*Maybe the chief is convinced that someone pushed me off the road. Why did Diane call me after we hadn't spoken for weeks? Maybe she feels her world crumbling around her.*

Putting on my coat, Stanley and I took a slow, short walk. The weather was cold, and the sun made my head hurt. "Okay, Stanley, let's get some rest."

I spent the rest of the day resting, sleeping, and playing a little with Stanley.

# Chapter 56

I tossed and turned most of the night, and I was happy to see the sunrise. My body hurt all over. I thought about calling off the trip to Denver, but I needed to finish what I had started.

Like clockwork, Ginny and Ron pulled up at nine. When I opened the garage door, Ginny opened her window.

She said, "Good luck. Say hello to Debbie for me."

I helped Stanley into the passenger seat and gave her a big smile. "I will. Thanks."

"I'm glad that you're driving, Ron. I hope that I'm not taking you away from too much business today."

"Will you stop apologizing? The more I think about what happened—and if the resort was at fault—then I want closure on this too. I'm here to back you up either way. Where are we going first?"

After picking up coffee and bagels with cream cheese, we went to Fred's Garage. My truck didn't look too bad. The left fender had been pushed in by a large rock, which had stopped me from going down further into the gully. Both front tires were flat, and the rims were bent. The damaged ball joints, steering coupling, sway bar, body panels, and paint were on order from the parts shop.

My insurance agent said he could arrange a rental car for me if I needed one. The engine and drive train hadn't suffered any damage, but they would still be checked. We walked to the rear of the car and saw two indentations just above the bumper.

*I am not an accident expert, but this shows me that this was no accident. Is that why the chief was looking for Brian's truck?*

Ron looked at the tailgate. "Mike, this wasn't an accident. You could have been killed!"

"You should have been there; it was a fast ride," I said with a smile.

I asked Fred to give me a call when he got the parts and a date when I could get the truck back.

"Okay, where to now?" Ron said.

"We need to get on the road, but I need to go to the bank first."

The clerk opened the vault for me.

I took the bolt out of the box and put it in to my backpack.

I think the clerk was relieved that the box felt lighter, but she just smiled at me.

"Let's go see Jack Evans. Debbie said she'd meet me in the lobby. It's located in the Seventeenth Street Plaza."

Ron dropped me off and went to pick up parts for a ski-tuning table at a dealer a few blocks away. "Mike, I think you'll be in good hands. Besides, Debbie can protect you just as well as I can," he said with a wink.

Since, Ron wasn't coming with me, I opened my backpack and took out the bolt. While he kept an eye on the road, I opened the flaps and brought it up for him to see.

He briefly looked at it and then at me. "When we rode up in the snow cat for the rescue, you asked me whether I had seen bolts on the tower base. I didn't pay attention, but you did. I feel bad that I can't back you up."

"Don't worry about it. At least this should shed some doubt on it being sabotage."

We arrived with thirty minutes to spare.

"Mike, since parking is at a premium, I'll stay at the dealer and pick you up when you call. Don't worry if you need to talk to Debbie a little longer. I'll be waiting for your call."

"Thanks. I'll call you. Wish me luck." I closed the door and walked to the building.

The waiting area had comfortable chairs and tables to the right of the main reception desk. To the left of the desk, security guards were checking packages. Everyone had to walk through a machine that resembled an airport scanner.

Debbie was reading papers that were spread out on a table. "I was just looking over some notes."

She was wearing diamond earrings that I had given her as a birthday gift. "Mike, are you alright?" as she hugged me.

"It must be the pain meds. It spaces me out a bit."

"I know. You never liked to take any meds.

"By the way, how's Stanley?"

"He's doing great, especially with all the attention he's getting from Ron and Ginny."

"Is Ron going to join us?"

"No, he needed to go supply shopping. He will pick me up when I call him."

"Does he still drive fast?"

"Yup, with his radar detectors on, I think we avoided three tickets. He and Ginny are a great help to me."

"I know. When you speak to Jack Evans, tell him about the computer system, the rescue, and the missing bolts. Please don't mention the e-mails directly. Let me work that into our conversation. If I feel that the conversation is getting a little too personal, I will let him know it."

"Okay. What about my accident?"

"I think they know about it because they already read Bob Trent's report. We'll play that one by ear. Let me call Jack's secretary to let her know we're ready to come up. Someone will come down and take possession of the bolt because we wouldn't be able to get it through security. Are you ready?"

"Let's do it." We stood up and walked toward the reception desk.

# Chapter 57

I took a deep breath as the elevator doors opened on the seventh floor.
Debbie introduced me to Jack's secretary.

She smiled and told us to have a seat for a few minutes.

*I wonder if anyone else would go as far as I am going. Now, I know what a whistleblower feels. Sometimes honest people step forward against a company's product or waste—and their lives become pure hell. They lose their jobs and their families.*

The secretary said that Mr. Evans was ready to see us and opened the door to his office.

Jack Evans stepped around his desk and shook hands with us. He smiled and asked us to take a seat on a leather couch.

Debbie put the folder on the table in front of us.

# Chapter 58

For an hour, I answered Jack's questions.

He asked how I had come into possession of the bolt and why I thought it belonged to the tower. He explained that the bolt would be sent to the FBI lab to determine whether it matched the tower base screw rods and the bolts found in Joe Crop's car. It would also determine whether there had been a failure of the bolt itself.

"Mike, the only issue I have is with Brian's threat. There were no other witnesses. That makes it your word against his."

"I guess my dog doesn't count, does he?"

"I wish he could. I can attest that my horses understand a lot of what I say, but unless they speak like Mr. Ed, I really can't use them in court." We all smiled. "I have been in contact with Chief Bob Trent, and he's forwarding his review of your accident. He's been working with the state police to determine whether someone did try to push you off the road and if that person was Brian Jones. A preliminary statement from Brian Jones said that he did admit to having a few beers at a friend's house and losing control of his vehicle while driving back to the resort on the same road. His vehicle went into a spin, but he doesn't remember hitting a vehicle. He certainly would have stopped. As you can gather from his statement, there wasn't an attempt to hurt you if in fact he did hit your vehicle."

"Unless there was a witness to his threats, the fact that he tried kill me is all circumstantial."

"Yes, even if his front and your rear bumpers match the impact point, the most we can hope for is leaving the scene of an accident," he said grimly.

"And the bolt?" I asked.

"His attorney will definitely say that you found bolts that were planted by PineTree or Mr. Crop."

*Why did I ever get involved? What the hell was I thinking? I even got Debbie into this mess. How stupid of me.*

"Mike, since the FBI has already been called into this case, they may want to contact you. I asked them to contact your attorney." Jack stood up, came around the table, and offered me his hand. "It has been a pleasure to meet you. Thank you for coming in today, especially after your accident, to discuss this tragedy. With your help, we may still be able to have a great ski season. You need to thank your attorney for her persistent efforts in contacting my office about all of this."

Jack shook hands with Debbie and thanked us again.

Debbie picked up some paperwork from his secretary and a statement for me to finish.

# Chapter 59

"I thought that went well, but there isn't a case. He did threaten me."

"I believe you. Otherwise, I wouldn't be putting my ass on the line. I'll go over everything again to see if we missed anything of consequence. I think you did extremely well under the circumstances. By the way, how are you feeling? Even though the couch was quite comfortable, I saw you shift your body a few times."

"To be honest, my back and legs do hurt. I am tired."

"I would like to sit down with you at a coffee shop, but under the circumstances, I think you need to rest. Here's the statement that needs to be filled out and signed by you. On top is my fax number. Fax it to me tonight or no later than noon tomorrow. Here's a self-addressed envelope that you can drop in the mailbox tomorrow. I attached the same outline I gave Jack, which should help you remember your thoughts from this morning."

"As usual, you're so organized. It will really help me get through this. I was a little uptight. Nothing like this has ever come across my life. After this is over, can we have dinner and talk about why we divorced? I know we somehow grew apart, but I'm not sure from what and—"

"I would like to have dinner with you to talk about what happened. I share the same thoughts that you are having. Before we can start new lives—or rekindle old ones—we need to talk about our feelings or anger. I guess we didn't do a good job."

"So it's a date?" I said.

"Yes, Michael Doyle, but I need to run—and you need to call Ron."

We hugged and kissed, and I watched her walk out of the building.

# Chapter 60

On the drive home, I filled in Ron about the meeting. I didn't really say what Debbie and I had discussed because Ron and Ginny had a lot of other things to think about without having my personal life cluttering their lives. *Maybe I just don't want to get everyone's hope up, including my own.*

"So even though Brian pushed you off the road, all this stuff is circumstantial unless there is a witness or he confesses to threatening you?"

"You got it, buddy."

"What's next?"

"If you don't mind, I am going to close my eyes and try to get some rest. Wake me up when we reach town."

"Sure. Sorry." Ron lowered the music, and I drifted off to sleep.

# *Chapter 61*

Ron woke me up when we pulled into town.

I said, "It would be wise of me to stop by the resort and pick up some of my personal stuff from the computer room."

"I thought you wanted us to ski a little on Squaw Run before the afternoon run disappears."

"You know me. If I could, I would. The resort is still paying me until the season officially ends. I don't know if my contract will be renewed for next season."

"Your dedication is noteworthy, but what if Brian or Joe are there? Wouldn't that be a little uncomfortable—or even unsafe?"

"Maybe. But I doubt that either one knows where I went this morning. If you don't mind, can you drop me off?"

"Sure. No problem. I need to run into the lockers and stop by the ski shop. Do you want to meet for lunch?"

"Sounds good." I stepped out of Ron's car and made my way to the administration building.

June was at her desk in the lobby. "I heard that you had an accident. Are you okay? That road is sometimes so icy that I try to avoid it if at all possible."

"Yes. The good news is that I am alive. But I still feel lousy."

"Shouldn't you be resting?"

"I will as soon as I pick up a few things from the computer room. By the way, is anyone here today?"

"No one at the moment, but Mr. Bunn was here in the morning. He left for the day."

"Okay. I shouldn't be long. And before you ask, Ron is driving me home."

I switched on the lights and logged into the management console. I checked the databases, and everything seemed to be fine. Running a few queries showed me that the databases and their backups were in sync. I logged into the third database I created before Joe Bunn and Brian started deleting records from it.

*Should I just delete it? I don't want to make any rash decisions because of how I feel at this moment. I'll just synchronize the most recent data from the primary database. Everything is up to date, and the third database has the older records.*

On the e-mail servers, I found some activity, but I really didn't care who was sending the e-mails. I felt better knowing that the system was working without problems, and I logged off.

I needed to replace the batteries in the cassette player. I picked it up, shut the door, and headed out to meet Ron.

# Chapter 62

"Ginny and I think you need rest. I am taking you home. Don't worry about Stanley. He'll be fine with us. We don't want to hear no for an answer. Got it?"

"I was going to ask you to take care of him until I am able to at least get on all fours to greet him."

"Good. He'll be fine. Now, if you need anything or are not feeling well, we expect you to call us."

"Yes, sir." I half-saluted him and thanked him again when we pulled up to my townhouse.

"I think you forgot something, this ancient cassette player, which reminds me that we need to add an iPod to your birthday list." He leaned over the passenger seat and handed it to me.

"Thanks Ron. It may be ancient, but it works."

As soon as I got into the house, I took another pain pill. It had been over six hours. I set the alarm for five, got undressed, and flopped into bed.

# Chapter 63

T he alarm scared the hell out of me, but I stayed in bed a little longer than usual. *Debbie looked so beautiful yesterday. Her smile was radiant. Maybe, we can work things out. The tasks at hand are important. I need to complete my statement.*

For the next hour, I wrote—and rewrote—my statement. After signing it, I took a slow walk up to the loft and prepared the fax cover letter with notations like "secret," "confidential," and "personal" written on it.

*That should get her attention—and everyone else in her office!*

While waiting for my breakfast to finish in the microwave, I saw my cassette player on the kitchen counter. I opened the back of the player and replaced the six AA batteries. I pushed the play button, but I heard no music. The cassette was finished on the one side.

*I probably didn't turn it off that eventful day when Brian Jones scared Stanley and me.* Reversing the cassette to about the middle, I pushed the start button. Santana started playing at the same time the microwave finished. Putting the player down, I grabbed my meal and tore off the plastic film.

Santana stopped playing, and I heard familiar voices. *Oh hell. That's my voice and Brian Jones. The threats he made to me were repeated verbatim. Holy shit! How is this possible? Who pushed the record button?*

I sat down at the kitchen nook. It was Stanley. It had to have been Stanley. I had been wearing earphones, but he must have hit the record button with his paw when I took the earphones off.

I played it two more times. Brian's threats were not scary anymore. I was exhilarated, and recharged. I immediately called Debbie.

# Chapter 64

"Debbie, can we talk?"

"Sure. I just picked up your secret fax. That sure got the attention of my office. Thanks a bunch."

"I thought that would wake up the office."

"Are you all right? Are you in danger?"

"No danger, just excited." I filled her in on what I discovered.

"You mean to tell me that Stanley recorded this conversation without either of you knowing it?"

"You bet he did!"

"The law in Colorado says that if you are taping a conversation with another person in this state—whether it is surreptitiously or not—you must inform that person that the conversation is being taped. Since Stanley can't speak, the taped conversation could be admitted in court. It's a stretch, but it may not come to it if Brian hears the tape."

"Brilliant, just brilliant. I just can't believe my luck."

"Have you given Stanley a big treat?"

"No. Stanley is with Ron and Ginny, but I will when I see him."

"Please hug him for me. Can you get that cassette tape and the player to me tonight or tomorrow morning?"

"Probably tomorrow morning. I'll ask Ron if he can deliver it to you."

"You need to rest. I'll call Ginny and speak with her. Someone will pick up that tape and the recorder from you. I'll take care of it."

"I need to call Jack's office as soon as we hang up. I need to make an addendum to your statement to include the tape and the recorder. Most likely, CBI will analyze it to determine that it wasn't doctored in any way."

"Is all this extra work going to cost me extra?"

"And to think I only asked you for a dollar retainer.

"What would you like from me besides money?"

"I would like the dinner you promised that we would have after all of this is done," she said without any hesitation.

# Chapter 65

Two days after Ron dropped off the tape and player with Debbie, I was still in pain. I wasn't doing well with the pain, especially in my neck. I was under strict orders from Ron and Ginny to rest and not get up at all. I felt helpless and missed Stanley. Ginny and Ron were taking turns dropping off Ginny's meals. I especially liked her homemade chicken soup.

I turned on the news and saw a reporter standing in front of the lodge. "I have learned that there was a startling reversal of the original investigation. Originally, the investigation focused on the lift being sabotaged by the eco-conservationist group PineTree. Local police and the FBI detained and repeatedly questioned Joe Crop from that group. However, we just found out from Chief Trent and the Elks Run Police Department that Joe Crop has been released and is no longer a suspect. I confirmed this information with Special Agent Jeff Peters who was assigned to the case because of the possible sabotage on Forest Service land.

"The investigators are now saying that Elks Run Resort may have been involved with the accident. There will be a live news conference at the city hall in one hour that will discuss this and other aspects of the investigation. We will be there covering it for you. Live from Elks Run in Summit County, Colorado, this is Joan Edwards, Eyewitness News 7."

"Thanks Joan, we will come back to you live in one hour."

I shut off the TV. How long had I been asleep? Everything had changed in the blink of an eye.

I heard the keys in the door, and Ron, Ginny, and Stanley rushed over to me.

I petted Stanley while he licked me over and over again. I was so happy to see him that I didn't even notice Debbie behind them.

"Debbie wanted to come along to see you," Ron said.

"Mike, if you need to know, they made me come—or I would have suffered the worst tongue-lashing this side of Loveland Pass," she said with a big smile. "I didn't come empty handed. I brought the wine to go with Ginny's lasagna and garlic bread."

"I am at a loss for words, which may be first. Let me open that bottle of wine while you guys set the table for this feast." I started pulling the cork. "With glasses held high, I would like to thank Ron and Ginny for being my friends for life, to Debbie for being my attorney, and a friend when I needed one, and Stanley who will get a few of Ginny's meatballs mixed in his dry food tonight. To all of you, let's toast!"

"Hear, hear."

We all raised our glasses.

# Chapter 66

As I reached for another piece of garlic bread, Debbie said, "The key to this whole mess is the tape. When Chief Trent played the tape to Brian and his attorney—coupled with the results of the paint from your truck and rear bumper matching the embedded chips found in his truck's front bumper—Brian broke down and admitted his involvement with Joe Bunn and Sky Stream. He also admitted setting up Joe Crop with those bolts."

"I assume that CBI found the tape genuine," I said.

"Yes. The tape was genuine, and since the FBI was brought into the investigation, Jack Evans asked them to check the bolt you dropped off to his office. The FBI found that the bolt and all the other bolts that Brian turned over matched the connecting rods of towers fourteen and fifteen. The FBI crime lab said that because the bolts were secured to the rods in extremely cold temperatures without proper insulation being put around those towers, the stress of running the lift caused minute cracks in them, probably when the season began at the resort. That led to the cracks, and the vibration of the towers caused them to collapse. There is a good possibility that other bolts would have failed, causing a bigger disaster. All the bolts on the lift will be replaced this summer."

"Joe told Brian to cover the towers after the fact. Did you need all the e-mails I saved?"

"No. When Brian started confessing, there wasn't any need to bring them into evidence. But, if he had a change of heart, I had them in my back pocket." She stood up to pour more wine.

"What's going to happen to Joe, Brian, and the others?" Ron asked.

"Will they go to jail?" Ginny asked.

"If my client wants to press charges against Brian for threatening him, he can, but I would advise him not to. Brian was facing a felony traffic offense for recklessly driving his vehicle into Mike's vehicle. However, since he has been very cooperative, he faces a misdemeanor offense of a class two that could land him in jail for up to a year and a $1,000 fine. He could be fined with court costs tacked on and be paroled with community service. And that's where Mike comes in."

I stood up and topped off everyone's glass.

"Mike will be called to appear in court and can make a recommendation to the judge as to what he would like the court to do since he was the wronged party. I haven't talked to Mike about his appearance, but I think I know what direction he will take," Debbie said with a smile.

"A fine and community work," I said after another sip of the wine.

"We all voted and thought that you would say that," Ron said with a smile.

"Since both of you have had a busy week, Ron and I will clean up this mess," Ginny said.

"Where's Stanley?" I asked.

"I think I saw him waddle to the bedroom," Ron said.

I carefully got down on my knees and approached his bed.

Stanley rolled onto his back for a belly rub.

Debbie touched my shoulder and asked if she could join the fun.

"You bet!" I said. "If we rub his belly and his ears, he'll be in hound heaven. Will I ever get my cassette recorder back?"

"You ask the silliest questions," she said with a big smile.

"Does this dinner mean we have to—"

"No, I want us to have a dinner by ourselves so we can talk about our divorce. I miss you and Stanley." She put her hand on mine.

"I, we, miss you too." I looked into her eyes and kissed her.

# Epilogue

T here were quite a few changes in the two and half years after we had Ginny's lasagna and garlic bread that night in March. After a number of dinners and walks with Stanley, including a few sessions with a marriage counselor, we got "un-divorced." The move to Colorado, Debbie's ambition to become a lawyer, and my insistence on starting my own business made us lose sight of "us." My mom was smiling again.

Debbie had expanded into real estate law and opened an office in Elks Run. She still worked part-time for the law firm in Denver from home, but she really wanted to succeed in her real estate practice. The area was growing by leaps and bounds, and many people wanted to move there. We were planning to move there from Denver. Believe it or not, I still had a contract to manage the computer systems at Elks Run.

Joe Bunn was working as a management consultant in California, and Diane moved back to Switzerland to take over as the marketing director at a Western Ventures resort. Brian Jones completed his community service and moved to Utah.

I impressed Jack Evans—with Debbie's help—and he recommended me for a contract managing the computer system for CBI's satellite office in Summit County. I stopped teaching snowboarding at Elks Run, but Debbie and I tried to sneak out during the season for a few quick runs down the slopes.

Christopher Doyle just turned eighteen months. Debbie and I took turns with Christopher; Mary, who still worked for Ron and Ginny, filled in when we needed a break.

Ron and Ginny were doing great and became Christopher's godparents. They opened a second store just outside of Elks Run that specialized in camping and water sports. Joe Crop is managing the store for them.

Stanley turned seven and started showing a little white on his muzzle. He was usually with Debbie in her office, with Ron and Ginny at one of their stores, or at home with Christopher and me. Christopher loved to cuddle up to Stanley and held onto him when he tried to stand.

Stanley will always be special to all of us.